The Dragon in Shallow Waters

The Dragon in Shallow Waters

V. Sackville-West

MINT EDITIONS

The Dragon in Shallow Waters was first published in 1921.

This edition published by Mint Editions 2021.

ISBN 9781513212166 | E-ISBN 9781513212067

Published by Mint Editions®

 MINT
EDITIONS

minteditionbooks.com

Publishing Director: Jennifer Newens
Design & Production: Rachel Lopez Metzger
Project Manager: Micaela Clark
Typesetting: Westchester Publishing Services

Contents

I	7
II	10
III	23
IV	32
V	38
VI	50
VII	60
VIII	68
IX	79
X	85
XI	103
XII	112
XIII	122
XIV	127
XV	132
XVI	143

I

An immense gallery, five hundred feet long, occupied the upper floor of the main factory-building. Looking down the gallery, a perspective of iron girders spanned the roof, gaunt skeletons of architecture, uncompromising, inexorably utilitarian, inflexible, remorseless. A drone of machinery filled the air, neither very loud nor very near at hand, but softly and unremittingly continuous; the drone of clanking, of loosely-running wheels and leather belts, muffled by the intervening floor into a not unpleasant murmur. Outside the windows three chimneys reared their heads side by side, emitting three parallel streams of smoke, gigantic black plumes that floated horizontally away over the flooded country, and that at night were flecked with red sparks as they flowed out from the red glare at their base.

All these things, the chimneys and the girders, were crushingly larger than the men who laboured amongst them. The men seemed of pigmy size as they pushed their hand-trucks along the floor of the big gallery. They pushed them down the narrow passage-ways left between the vats. The gallery was full of vats, set in pairs down the whole length of the building; square vats twenty feet each way, as large and as deep as an ordinary room. Some of the vats were empty, temporarily not in use; some were only half full; but in most the hot, liquid soap boiled and bubbled right up to the rim.

The smell which filled the gallery was the smell of the soap, pungent and acrid on the surface, but fat and nauseating underneath, rasping the throat of the chance visitor before it penetrated deeper with its hot, furry smell that tickled and disgusted the sensitiveness at the back of his nose. The chance visitor rarely lingered long in the gallery. He would stand for a few moments watching the men that came and went in their splashed overalls, indifferent to his presence; then he would turn to go carefully down the steep iron stair into the pleasanter rooms where white powder was heaped on the floor in miniature mountains, and where lines of girls seated on high stools were occupied in tying ribbons with the twist of dexterity round the necks of scent bottles, and the room was filled with scent like a garden of orange-trees in blossom.

Up in the gallery, the soap in the vats moved uneasily with the motion of an evil quicksand. The soap was yellow, and its consistency one of slimy liquidity. If the vat were not sufficiently full, the quantity increased mysteriously from below, the level rising thanks to the unseen source of supply. It was not hard to believe that the recesses of the vat were inhabited by some foul and secret monster whose jaws emitted the viscid, yellow stream to conceal his abode. The soap moved restlessly, boiling and bursting into little craters, which subsided, leaving wrinkles and circles on the surface. Quiet for a moment, it heaved in another place; heaved slowly and deliberately, but did not break; heaved again; broke with a spout of steam and a sluggish splash as the walls of the crater fell in. It was never altogether still. It seemed alive, because it swelled and breathed and vomited, or at least it seemed as though some live creature dwelt within, occasioning by its movements the disturbances and eruptions of the slime.

In other vats a wrinkled brown skin had formed over the cooling soap, a skin puckered and broken up into valleys and chasms, plains and ridges, so that of all things it most resembled the physical map of a country. The parallel was exact as to colour, even to the greenish stretches at the bottom of the valleys. Mountain ridges three inches high, chasms three inches deep, plateaux six inches across, the landscape of some dead but perpetually changing world. For here the slime moved also, but with a difference; it did not seethe, it did not erupt; it rather subsided; was a dead, rather than a living thing. The monster that dwelt in those depths had died, and lay at the bottom, a heap of corruption the imagination would not willingly picture.

Other vats were empty, and if the hot boiling soap resembled a shifting quicksand, and the cooling soap the desolation of a dead world, the empty vats resembled the sea-bottom. The others, with their hint of greed and evil, might be more terrifying; these empty vats were infinitely more fantastic. Their sides were caked with the dry soap, brown-yellow, and their depths were surprisingly revealed; ending in a blunt point, like the point of a cone; they were sunk lower than the floor of the gallery into an unlighted chamber of corresponding size below. In these empty vats, various portions of apparatus were brought to light: immense chains, caked and corroded, hung like ship's cables and were lost in the deposit at the bottom; vast strainers swung against the sides; ropes, stiffened hard as wood, spanned diagonally from side to side; and, emerging from the tapering depths, stumps of wreckage stood up, transformed from their original shape to stalagmites of dry frangible matter, that would chip away, crisp and powdery, betraying the nature of their kernel,—was it a shovel? was it an anchor? was it the decaying bones of the ancient monster?—and the low parapets of the vats were coated with the same brittle dryness that yellowed the walls of those grotesque and extraordinary pits.

II

I

THE WORKERS WERE SUBORDINATE TO the factory; it was a giant, a monster, that they served. At night the red glow from the chimneys,—the glow from the fires that must never flag or die,—accentuated the disregard of man's convenience. To keep alive that red breath of activity, men must forego their privilege of sleep.

The tragedy in the household of the Denes was not allowed to interrupt the general work of the factory, but the overseer, Mr. Calthorpe, offered Silas Dene a week, and Gregory Dene a day,—the day of the funeral,—as a concession to their mourning. He thought the offer sufficiently generous.

The brothers Dene, however, refused it.

They lived in a double-cottage; Gregory with his wife in one half; Silas and his wife, before her sudden death, in the other. Although situated in the village street, it was a lonely cottage, for "the black Denes" did not encourage neighbourly communion, nor did the neighbours trouble them with unwelcome advances. This was not surprising, for they were indeed a sinister race to whom affliction seemed naturally drawn. Nature cursed them from the hour of their birth with physical deficiencies and spiritual savagery; whether or no, as some said, the latter was only to be expected as the outcome of the former, the name of Dene remained the intimidation of the village.

Others again said that Nature was not so much to be held responsible as the Denes' father, whom everybody had known as a rake, and who never ought to have married, much less begotten children.

Of the two brothers, Gregory had been deaf and dumb from birth, and Silas blind. Their physique, however, was full of splendour, and they were accounted two of the most valuable workers in the factory,—magnificent men, tall, muscular, and dark.

Calthorpe came to their cottage directly he was told of the accident. It was then evening, and the accident had occurred in the earlier part of the afternoon. Calthorpe knew no details beyond the bare fact that Silas Dene's wife had been discovered, a mass of almost unidentifiable disfigurement, lying across the railway line after the passage of the little local train. He had been told this much by the men who had come running with the news to his office; they had come breathless, shocked, mystified; he had understood at once that they were mystified; they had made no comment, but Calthorpe had been quick to catch the hint of mystery; any concern of the Denes was always luscious with mystery.

He found Silas, the blind man, sitting in his kitchen, chewing an unlighted pipe. He appeared to be strangely indifferent. A little man named Hambley, Silas Dene's only crony, sat in a dark corner, not speaking, but observing everything with bright furtive eyes, like the eyes of a weasel. He hugged himself in his corner; a sallow faced little man, with a red tip to his thin nose. Gregory Dene was in the kitchen too, and Gregory's wife, with frightened eyes, was laying the table for supper; she moved quickly, placing cups and plates, and casting rapid glances at the two men.

"I'm terribly distressed, Silas," Calthorpe began.

"What, you too, Mr. Calthorpe, come to condole?" cried the blind man, laughing loudly. "Well, it takes an accident to make me popular, it seems; I haven't had so many callers in the last four years as in the last four hours. Sit down, Mr. Calthorpe; I ask 'em all to sit down. Nan, give a chair."

Calthorpe sat down uneasily, beneath the silent scrutiny of Gregory and the quick glances of Gregory's wife. The burning and sightless eyes of Silas were also bent upon him.

"I have only just heard the news," he began again, "or I would have come sooner. . ."

"That's all right. The neighbours ran to help, and to nose out what they could; the parson came too, he's upstairs now. All very helpful," said Silas, with another burst of laughter. "Gregory, my brother, too, though he isn't much company, but we understand one another. Don't we, Gregory? He can't hear, but I always talk to him as though he could. I trust him with my secrets, Mr. Calthorpe. They say dead men tell no tales; I say deaf and dumb men tell no tales either. We understand one another, don't we, Gregory?" He looked without seeing at the deaf mute who had listened without hearing, aware only that Silas was speaking by the movement of his lips. "One's always sorry to have told a secret," Silas said, nodding at Calthorpe; "always sorry sooner or later, but Gregory, my brother, he's safe with any secret. I only tell them to him. Never to Nan, and I never told one to Hannah. Only to Gregory. All my secrets," and he fell silent, and began biting his lips, pressing them between his teeth with his fingers, that were surprisingly long and nervous.

Calthorpe did not know how to answer; he looked at Gregory's wife, trying to establish a bond of helpful sympathy between himself and her, the two normal people in that room, but she immediately looked away in her scared and nervous fashion. Calthorpe then saw that Gregory was watching him with a malicious sarcasm that startled Calthorpe for a moment into the belief that he was actually grinning, although no grin was there. Thus startled, he began to speak, hurriedly, confining himself to the practical.

"Of course, you must take sometime off, Silas; this week will be very trying for you, and very busy too; there will be the inquest and the funeral." ("Why did I say that?" he thought to himself.) "We shall all want to make it as easy as possible for you, and the men will be glad to take turns at your job. You mustn't worry about that. Supposing I give you a week?" Seeing that Silas's lips curled with what he took to be disdain, he thought that perhaps his offer had been inadequate, and added to it, "and your brother of course would be given the day of the funeral, and if at any other time you want him, Silas, you have only to ask me; I shouldn't be hard on you."

"We don't want anytime off," Silas replied ungraciously.

"You know that it is customary. . ." said Calthorpe. Customary! he clung to the word; it gave him a sense of security. "It is customary," he repeated, "in the case of death, or sickness, or accident, to release such near relatives as are employed at the factory. You needn't think you would be accepting a special favour."

"Why should I think that, Mr. Calthorpe?"

Calthorpe knew from the instant defiance in the blind man's tone that he must make no allusion to Silas's disability; he said, "Well, the sad circumstances of your wife's death. . ."

"She brought me my dinner as usual," said Silas suddenly; "she sat with me in the shed while I ate it, down by the railway, like she always did, because afterwards she used to bring me back to my work, and then carry the plate and things home. Just like every other day. When I'd done she took me back and left me in the shops; I didn't know anything more. After I'd been there two or three hours they came and told me. They said she'd been found on the railway line. I don't know how long she'd been there, or why she didn't start off for home at once. Perhaps she'd been waiting for the fog to lift; there was a fog today, wasn't there? and anyway I could feel it in my breath without her telling me so. It was extra thick down on the railway. Perhaps she waited for it to lift. Or perhaps she was waiting to meet somebody in the shed."

"Waiting to *meet* somebody, Silas?"

"I'm a blind man, Mr. Calthorpe, and she was a blind man's wife."

Calthorpe saw that Gregory's wife had ceased her little clatter with the supper-things, and was standing as though stupefied beside the supper table, her fingers resting on its edge. Now she moved again, setting a kettle on the range.

"I knew nothing till hours after she left me—two or three hours," Silas reverted. "Nothing until they came and told me. I'd been working all the afternoon. She left me at the door of the shops, Mr. Calthorpe," he said; "she didn't come in with me."

"No, no; I see," said Calthorpe.

"Sometimes she'd come in for a chat; she was friendly with my mates, friendly with Donnithorne specially. He'd come here sometimes, Sundays, wouldn't he, Gregory? But today she didn't come in. No. She said she had a bit of mending to do at home; that's it, a bit of mending. She wanted to get home quick."

"Then why should you think she waited to meet anybody in the shed?" asked Calthorpe.

"That's only my fancy; I'm a blind man, Mr. Calthorpe; I couldn't have seen who she waited for, or who she met. Gregory could have seen. But *I* couldn't, and Gregory wasn't there. You know he works inside the factory, Mr. Calthorpe, and I work in the shops down by the railway-sheds, tying up the boxes."

"I know; you're a grand worker," said Calthorpe. He was afraid of Silas. He saw with relief that the clergyman had come down from the upper room, and was standing on the lowest step of the stairs where they opened into the kitchen.

"I knew nothing," Silas went on with a rising voice. "Funny, that a man's wife should be lying across railway lines, and the man not know it. Husband and wife should be one, shouldn't they? But I never told her my secrets. Women don't understand men's secrets. I don't hold with women, Mr. Calthorpe, they're lying and deceitful animals; you can't trust them out of your sight, and as I haven't any sight it stands to reason I can't trust them at all. But husband and wife should be one all the same, so they say. Dutiful and patient and faithful, that's what women ought to be, but they're only artful. Perhaps I'll be better without one. I'll get a man to share the house with me, and lead me about when I need it; I know a nice young chap who'd be glad."

II

"My poor friend, your sorrow has thrown you off your balance," said the clergyman as he came forward and laid his hand upon Silas's shoulder.

"That's you, Mr. Medhurst?" said Silas, instantly recognising the voice, which indeed was unmistakable. "You've prayed over her; well, I hope she's the better for it. Heaven send me a parson to pray over me when my turn comes, that's all I say."

"My poor friend," the clergyman said again, "pray rather to Heaven now that you be not embittered by your affliction. Let us call forth our courage when the test comes upon the soul; let us pray to be of those whose courage is steadfast even unto death. The lot of man is trouble and affliction, and He in His Mercy hath appointed our courage as the weapon wherewith to meet it."

"That's a help, isn't it, Mr. Calthorpe?" said Silas, "that's a great help, that thought. Is that what you say, Mr. Medhurst, to a man that's going to the gallows? What do you tell him—to feel kindly towards his jailers, the judge who condemned him, the jury that found him guilty, the police that arrested him, the man or woman he murdered, the teacher that taught him, the mother that bore him, and the father that begot him? You tell him not to curse them all,—eh? You tell him to feel kindly and charitable like you've told me to be long-suffering under my blindness and to have courage now my wife's dead,—eh? you tell him that?"

"I am not a prison chaplain, Dene," said Mr. Medhurst, stiffly, removing his hand which, however, he immediately replaced, saying with compassion, "My poor friend, my poor friend! you are sorely tried."

"There's worse things than death, Mr. Medhurst," Silas exclaimed, and he sprang up as though the clergyman's touch were unendurable to him, and stood in front of the range, having felt his way rapidly across the room. Mr. Medhurst followed him, but Silas heard him coming, and moved away again, behind the table. Mr. Medhurst turned to Calthorpe with a gesture of resignation, saying in a low voice, "These poor fellows! we must be tolerant, Calthorpe," and Gregory continued to watch the movements and gestures, which he could understand, although he could not hear their speech. "Look here, sir," Silas began again, "I didn't know of the accident, not till hours afterwards, as I've been telling Mr. Calthorpe,—is Mr. Calthorpe still here?"

"Yes, Silas, I'm still here," said the overseer.

"Ah, I thought I hadn't heard the door. Well, I was in the shops, and they told me at five o'clock. When they came to tell me, I asked what time it was, and they told me, five o'clock. Now it was two o'clock when I finished my dinner; I asked Hannah, and she told me, two o'clock. That's three hours, sir. Mark that. She'd been on that line three hours before her husband knew it. Is that right, when husband and wife should be one?"

"They told you directly she was found, Dene," said the clergyman. "No one is to blame."

"I'm blaming no one," said Silas sullenly, "I only ask you to mark it, sir: three hours. Three hours before I knew."

"Why does he insist on that point?" thought Calthorpe.

"I'm alone now, a lonely man and a blind one. The inquest now,— must you have an inquest?"

"We are all equal before the law," said Mr. Medhurst in a gentle and reproving voice.

"And I have to go to it?"

"I am afraid so, Dene."

"Well, I'll tell them what I told you: it was three hours before I knew. She was alive at two o'clock, when she left me," said Silas with great violence, striking his fist upon the table and glaring round the room with his sightless eyes; "you've all heard: three hours,—you, Mr. Medhurst, and you, Mr. Calthorpe, and you, Hambley, and you, Nan. Come here, Nan."

Gregory's wife went to him, like a dog to a cruel master; he had thrust his fingers through his black hair, and looked wild. He groped for her shoulder; clutched it firmly.

"Tell Gregory, Nan; tell him she had been dead three hours before I knew."

Gregory's wife made swift passes with her fingers to her husband, who read the signs and answered in the same language.

"He says you told him that when you first came in, Silas." She had a clear and gentle voice.

"You hear that, Mr. Medhurst? you hear, Mr. Calthorpe? I told my brother that when I came in. I'm alone now; I had a son, but I don't know where he is; I had a daughter too, but she went soon after her brother. I stand alone; I don't count on nobody."

"Come, Dene; I respect your sorrow, but I cannot hear you imply that your children deserted you: you were always, I am afraid, a harsh father." Mr. Medhurst spoke in the reprimanding tone that he could assume at a moment's notice; it was shaded with regret, as though he spoke thus not from a natural inclination to find fault, but from a pressure of duty.

"Why don't you say that I was harsh to Hannah?" demanded Silas. Mr. Medhurst made a deprecatory movement with his hands; he would not willingly bring charges against a man already in trouble. "Why don't you say so?" repeated the blind man, upon whom the movement was naturally lost.

"Since you insist," said the clergyman, "I must say that the whole village knew you were not always very kind to your wife; in fact, I have spoken to you myself on the subject."

"I knocked her about; I'd do the same to any woman, if I was fool and dupe enough to take up with another one," Silas said.

His pronouncement left the room in silence; his blind glare checked the words on the lips of both the clergyman and the overseer; he still stood entrenched behind the table, his sinewy hand gripping Nan's small shoulder, for she dared do nothing but remain motionless, neither cowering away nor moving closer to him, but keeping her eyes bent upon the floor. An oil-lamp swung from the ceiling above the table. Gregory watched them all in turn, from his chair beside the oven; he was really grinning now, and seemed more in the mood to defend his brother's quarrels with his fist than to take any interest in the visible terror of his wife. Nor did she appear to expect championship from him. She had not thrown him so much as one appealing glance. Living between the two brothers, she might almost have forgotten which of the two was her husband and which her brother-in-law; in fact, it had been whispered in the village that the mode of life in the Denes' cottage was such as to lead the woman into that kind of confusion,—but those who spoke so were the ignorant, who disregarded or else knew nothing of the pride and jealousy of the Denes.

"I didn't knock her about so cruelly as the train," said Silas, laughing wildly.

"O Lord!" Mr. Medhurst began, clasping his hands, "look with mercy upon this Thy servant, that in the hour of his trial. . ."

"Trial? what's that?" cried Silas. "An inquest isn't a trial, that I'm aware?"

". . . that in the hour of his trial he may rise above the sorrows of the flesh to a more perfect understanding of Thy clemency. . ."

V. SACKVILLE-WEST

"It's just babble," said Silas, who was shaking now with rage from head to foot.

"Save him, O Lord, from the mortal sin of profanity; endow him with strength righteously to live, bringing him at the last out of the sea of peril into the calm waters of that perfect peace. . ."

"You so smooth and righteous, sir, I wonder it doesn't shock you to see a woman battered in like Hannah's battered now; yet you went and said your prayers over her; fairly gloated over her, perhaps?"

"Look, O Lord, with mercy upon this Thy poor distraught but faithful servant. Consider him with leniency; mercifully pardon. . ."

"Look here," Silas cried, "the Lord'll hear your prayers just as well if they're put up from your parsonage. This is my cottage, and my affairs are my affairs; what I do, or what's sent to me, and how I take it, is my affair. I've always held that a man was a thing by himself, specially when he's in trouble; he isn't forced to be the toy of sympathy, and of help he doesn't want. Let me alone. I don't want your prayers, Mr. Medhurst. I don't want your holiday, Mr. Calthorpe. I'll be at my work tomorrow morning same as I always am—same as I was today after my wife died, though, mark you, I didn't know it. I don't whine, so I don't want you to do my whining for me. No. I never missed a day at my work yet, and though I'm blind I work to keep myself, and I'll look after myself, and my rights, blind as I am,—I'll not be deceived, not I 'Poor blind Silas.' Don't let me hear you say that. Perhaps I know more than you think, and guess the rest." He went off into a string of mumblings, and a slight foam of saliva appeared at the corners of his mouth.

"It's no good staying here, Mr. Medhurst," said Calthorpe, trying to get the clergyman away.

"You speak to him, Calthorpe."

"I'll try.—Here, Silas, you don't hate me?" said Calthorpe, going up to the blind man.

"No; you're a well-meaning, ordinary sort of chap," replied Silas.

"Yes, I don't want to be anything else. Now see here, if you think work will keep your mind off things, you must come to work; but if you want to stop away, you can stop away for a week. Is that clear?"

"I'll come to work. A man's got a right to decide for himself, hasn't he?"

"Of course he has; but don't be too hard on yourself. Don't get mulish. You don't look right somehow. You're all out of gear; small wonder just now, but you know as well as I do that you're a bit ill-balanced at the best of times. Take it easy, Silas."

"You mean well, I dare say."

"Yes, I swear I do; don't say it so grudgingly. See here: cling on to your political grievances, man; they'll take your mind off your own troubles."

"I know how to bear my own troubles."

"I'm only giving you a hint; get angry over something. Go down and make one of your speeches to the debating society. I don't share your views, and I disapprove of your methods, because they stir up trouble amongst the men, but I'd like to think that something was helping you."

"Chatter!" said Silas suddenly.

"You're too damned scornful," said Calthorpe flushing. "All right then; fight it out with yourself. Snarl at your mates, and scare the women. Make yourself lonelier than you already are, you poor lonely devil."

Silas laughed at that, and some of the hostility went out of his face.

"Thanks, Mr. Calthorpe. I'll be at work tomorrow. Going now?"

"Mr. Medhurst and I are both going—unless you want us to stay?"

"No, I don't want you to stay."

"No ill-feeling, Silas?"

"None, if you mean because you mislaid a bit of your temper."

III

NAN OPENED THE DOOR FOR Mr. Medhurst and Calthorpe, who passed out together and were immediately lost to sight in the fog. In the winter months, fog hung almost continuously over that low, fenny country; white fog; billowy, soaking mist. Little wraiths of it swirled into the kitchen as she opened the door, so she shut it again quickly,—she did everything quickly and neatly. For one moment of panic she wished she could have gone with Calthorpe, who was kindly, commonplace, and easy, instead of remaining alone with those two violent and difficult men, and the dead body of her sister-in-law upstairs. She was weary of the strain that never seemed to be relaxed in their cottage.

"Next time that canting parson comes here, I'll lay hands upon him," said Silas.

"Will I get supper now?" asked Nan, trying to distract him.

"What a packet of folk we had!" Silas broke out; "it was rat-tat at the door all the time, till the whole village had passed through, I should say."

"Folks are kindly," said Nan.

"Folks are curious," barked Silas.

She sighed, but, knowing better than to remonstrate, resumed her question.

"Will you have supper now, Silas?" and she repeated the question on her fingers to Gregory. "We'll eat with you, Silas, tonight. Gregory and I,—we'll be there whenever you want us. I'll do the house for you, and your cooking. We'll all eat together, so long as you want us to." She was gentle and bright.

"I don't want your pity."

She busied herself with getting the supper out of the oven, carrying the hot dishes carefully with a cloth. Gregory watched her, pivoting in his chair to follow her movements. Once he talked to her on his fingers: "Don't you take no notice of Silas; he looks queer tonight," and when she answered, "Small wonder," a broad grin distorted his dark face. His bones and features, strongly carven, in conjunction with the muscularity of his body and the perpetual silence to which he was condemned, made him appear like a man cast in bronze. He was, moreover, singularly still; he would sit for hours without stirring, his arms folded across his chest; he never betrayed what he was thinking, but the others knew that it was always about machinery. Silas, on the other hand, was far more excitable; he was always occupied; his mind had many trains of thought which it pursued; Nan never knew which of the two brothers she found the more alarming, and life had become for her an uneasy effort to conciliate them both. She had hesitated before speaking of supper; meals seemed to accord badly with tragedy.

Silas talked unceasingly; he talked with his mouth full and many phrases were unintelligible. Now and then he mumbled, now and then raised his voice to a shout. He thundered assertions, and spat questions at Nan. Gregory sat crumbling bread and sneering at her distress. She was distressed because Silas was in one of his most uproarious moods, launching opinions on his diverse subjects, everyone of which readily attained the proportions of an obsession in his mind; and she was distressed further because she had all the while the alienating sensation that her husband understood his brother better than she did, although he could hear no word. She sat between them, eating very little, while they ate voraciously. She was thinking of Hannah, who lay upstairs.

Once she asked a question. "Who'll you get, Silas, to live with you now?"

"Linnet Morgan. He's anxious to find handy lodgings."

"Linnet Morgan. That's the chap newly in charge of the scents? Would he live with just working-people like us?"

"What's the difference?"

Nan could not define it. She had not intended a challenge, but Silas had a trick of treating everything as a challenge.

"He's soft," she said at last.

"He'll learn not to be soft here."

Towards the end of the supper, Silas fell into one of his silences that were little less alarming than his speech. He sat over the range, chewing his pipe. Nan, having cleared away the supper, made herself small with some sewing in a corner. Gregory, looming hugely about the low room, disposed his drawings on the table under the direct light of the hanging lamp. They were on oiled paper, pale blue, pale pink, and white; large sheets of exact drawings of exquisitely intricate machinery. He bent over them, handling pencils, rulers, small compasses, and other neat instruments of his craft with a certain and delicate touch. He had clamped the drawings to the table with drawing pins, holding down the curling corners, smoothing out the shine of the folds. He was lost at once in them, forgetting both his own observant mockery and the tragedy which had seized and shaken his relations in its rough grasp. He was lost in his silent world of smooth-sliding precision and perfection.

His drawing was his hobby, not his profession; he guarded it from the outside world as a secret, and in the factory perversely clung to the meanest and most strenuous physical labour. When his wife protested—with more politeness than indignation—his fingers ran in emphatic oaths. When his machines were ripe to be shown, he would lay them before the whole board of directors; yes, he would startle those gentlemen; but until then he would be a workman, wheeling the barrels of liquid soap to the vats, beating and stirring it in the vats when it needed cooling,—nothing more.

He worked under the light of the lamp, making here a dot of correction, there a measurement of infinitesimal exactitude. His great fingers touched as delicately as those of a painter of miniatures.

The kitchen clock ticked in the stillness.

IV

NAN ROSE PRESENTLY, HEAPING HER sewing into her large open basket. Her husband was still absorbed in his drawings, and Silas in his meditations, over which he muttered and scowled. He seemed to be conducting an argument with himself, for his lips moved, he nodded or shook his head, and tapped his fingers upon his knee. Nan hesitated before disturbing him. But she knew that she must warn him before she left the room, for he could communicate with Gregory only with difficulty. She put her hand on his shoulder.

"Eh? what's that?" said Silas, starting; he had been very deeply lost in his thoughts.

"I'm going to our cottage for a bit, Silas, to put things straight there; I'll be back presently."

"Gregory's here, isn't he?"

"Yes, he's got his drawings out on the table."

Silas grunted, and Nan, after wrapping a muffler round her head and mouth, let herself out of the front door.

In her own kitchen, which was identical with Silas's in the other half of the cottage, she stood breathing with a sense of relief. Ah! if she might remain there! But she might not; Silas, who fought all the time against her sympathy and her ministrations, Silas, in spite of that ungracious ferocity, was now dependent upon her and could not be forsaken. Responsibilities by a cruel irony thrust themselves upon her weakness. She, who had so much need of protection, must protect.

She must not idle here.

She began rapidly clearing away the disorder of the day, raking out the fire, and drawing the short curtains across the little windows. She took her husband's boots into the scullery at the back of the kitchen, and set them ready to be cleaned the next morning. She went upstairs with a candle, turned down the bed, drew the curtains there too, and tidied the dressing-table. Through the partition in the next cottage was, she knew, a similar bedroom, and in that bedroom, where Silas and Hannah had slept every night for twenty-five years and where Hannah's two children had been born, the remains of Hannah now lay, covered over with a sheet, and Hannah, brawny, loud-voiced, tyrannical towards her sister-in-law, bullied by Silas, at times sullen and at times nosily recalcitrant towards him, would no longer go about the house as a working-woman, her sleeves rolled up, an apron over her dress, clattering pails and mops, ordering stray children off her whitened doorstep. Nan had not loved Hannah, but she thought it horrible that Hannah should be lying through that thin partition, in the disfigurement of which the men had whispered.

She wished that she dared arrange to sleep in another room, but Gregory would be angry.

She finished her work as quickly as she could and returned to Silas's cottage; only a couple of yards separated front-door from front-door, but, shivering, she pressed her muffler against her mouth to keep out the fog. The light and warmth were welcome again as she slipped into the kitchen.

Silas had not heard her. Gregory had his back to the door and did not see her. He was still bending over his drawings, all unaware that Silas stood near him, speaking, a wild and reckless look upon his face.

"You can't hear me, Gregory, old man. Old brother Gregory, wrapped up in your drawings! How much do you know, hey? How much do you guess? *I* did it—you know that, hey? She laughed at me—with Donnithorne. She played the dirty on me—with Donnithorne. I hated her, but I've got my honour to look after. I shan't tell anybody, only you, old man. Tell you I did it—hey? Don't tell anybody, Gregory!"

III

I

CALTHORPE AND MR. MEDHURST HAD ENTERED into a conspiracy to spare Silas from attending the inquest.

As they walked away from the Denes' cottage together, in the fog, they did not speak for sometime. They were turning the same thoughts over in their minds as they paced side by side down the village street, seeing the lights in the windows on either hand very dimly through the fog. The lantern which Calthorpe carried, swaying, lit up a pale milky circle but cast no forward ray. They were chilled; little drops of moisture gathered on the clergyman's eyebrows and on Calthorpe's brown beard; their very footfalls seemed to be muffled by the fog.

"It was warmer in Dene's kitchen, Calthorpe!" said the clergyman at last, handling his chilblained fingers tenderly, and then beating his hands together in their thick woollen gloves.

"Yes, sir, but I'd sooner be out here than in that unhealthy sort of atmosphere,—like that poor little woman. I think, if you ask me, the fog was thicker in that room than it is out here. I scarcely liked to come away leaving her there. I never saw anyone look more out of place. And so resigned, too; never a thought of revolt. But not glum, not pulling a long face; that's what touched me."

"No doubt she enjoys sufficient philosophy and religion to accept with a brave fortitude the lot she has herself chosen," said Mr. Medhurst.

Calthorpe, who had been feeling slightly exalted and full of a chivalrous emotion, the novelty of which surprised him agreeably, thought that Mr. Medhurst laid hands of lead upon a butterfly.

"Well, I thought there was something *lighter* about her than that, somehow," he said, struggling; but as the clergyman remained rigid, with a compassionate murmur of "Poor soul!" he turned to another subject. "Silas Dene seemed more excitable than usual, sir; they are strange fellows, those two, and you never know how they are going to take things. Silas's readings work upon his mind; he's full of queer theories. No doubt you've noticed, Mr. Medhurst. First he's off on one hobby-horse, and then another. Politics, death, women, fate, science, even poetry—he's got his views on them all; not lukewarm views, or ready to listen to argument, as you or I might be, but loud, aggressive views, and contradiction only makes him angry. He fairly bullies the village; I don't know how he does it, but all the chaps are too much afraid of him to turn upon him." Calthorpe came at last with a rush to the real point he had in sight, and said, "I thought his manner more than usually queer tonight; queerer, I mean, even than the circumstances warranted?"

"Yes; his irreverence—I might almost say his blasphemy—was very painful to hear; but we must remember, he is sorely tried."

Calthorpe grunted.

"I wasn't considering it, sir, only from the point of view of the church," he suggested.

They had reached the little gate leading to the Rectory, and Mr. Medhurst stood with his hand on the latch. The breath of the two men eddied like smoke in the fog above the pallid light of Calthorpe's lantern. Mr. Medhurst repressed his desire for the shelter of his own study, inhospitable as it was; so faint a stirring could scarcely be dignified by the name of desire, but such as it was he repressed it, recognising an enemy; personal inclinations were allowed no place in a life of monotonous mortification; his conscience ordered him to remain out in the raw evening until Calthorpe had finished saying whatever he might have to say, so he remained. Suavity, patience, tolerance, impartiality; above all, no self-indulgence.

"Yes, Calthorpe?" he prompted.

"That man's not in a fit state to attend an inquest," the overseer brought out.

"Ah. No, perhaps not," said Mr. Medhurst, and then, startled, "You don't mean. . ."

"Good gracious, sir, I don't mean anything,—only to spare the man. It's a clear enough case of accident," muttered Calthorpe. "I'm only afraid he'll lose his head if he's brought to the inquest; begin to rant on all his pet topics, do himself harm very likely; be talked about; give a bad name to the factory; perhaps lose his job. The Board is very particular. And I can't help having a liking for Silas Dene; he's a sound worker, he's full of pluck, he doesn't drink as many men would under his circumstances. I can't help having a respect for the man. He's something out of the ordinary. Can't we keep him away from the inquest, Mr. Medhurst?"

"Unfortunately, he was the last person to see his wife alive."

"I think I can get round the coroner, sir, if you'll back me up." Calthorpe was quite eager.

"I will certainly lend you my support," said the clergyman rather dubiously. "After all, it is a clear case of accident, as you say, and the inquest will only be a formal affair. I suppose it is really a clear case," he added, "but his manner was very peculiar."

"There now, sir," said Calthorpe, pouncing on him, delighted to have proved his point, "you know Silas Dene as well as I do, and we both trust him, yet, having seen him in this state, you're aware of the beginnings of doubt; what about the coroner, who comes out from Lincoln, and has never heard of Dene or his record before? I tell you, we must keep the man away. It's only decent, only Christian. The man's blind in more ways than one; we must see for him, and keep him from hitting his head against a wall."

"No doubt you are right; I'll help you. Send for me when you want me, Calthorpe; goodnight."

"Goodnight, sir; thank you."

Calthorpe hurried away with his lantern into the fog; Mr. Medhurst let himself in at his front door. He wondered whether he had been too hasty in leaving Calthorpe, whether he ought not to have inquired more thoroughly into the overseer's exact meanings. Had his wish for creature comfort relaxed the vigilance he kept over his conscience? In any case, it was too late now for regrets. With a sigh he laid his coat, his clerical hat, his muffler and his gloves on the sideboard in his narrow hall, and, passing into his study, held a match to the gas-jet above his table. A small pop of explosion resulted in a thin blue flame. No fire burnt in the grate; Mr. Medhurst never permitted himself a fire until seven o'clock in the evening, and by the clock he saw that it was only half-past six. He blew upon his fingers, trying to warm them. For a few moments he knelt in prayer for guidance at his black horsehair sofa, then, rising, he drew his chair up to the writing-table and began to deal, methodically, with a pile of his papers. He had pigeon-holed Silas Dene already in the files of his mind.

II

SILAS DENE CAME TO THE inquest in spite of Calthorpe's intervention, Mr. Medhurst's collaboration, and the coroner's acquiescence.

He had agreed not to come; he had been surly and ungracious, but finally had given his consent and had even added a word of conventional gratitude. He had given a written affidavit, which was read at the inquest before his arrival. All evidence had been taken, that of Dene's mates, of the driver of the truck-train,—the fog had been very thick at the level-crossing, and he couldn't see five yards ahead of him,—that of the shunters who had found the body lying across the rails. All had gone smoothly in unbroken formality; the inquest was held in the village concert-room, with the body lying next door; Calthorpe was there, Mr. Medhurst, a representative of the board of directors, and many of the factoryhands who out of curiosity had interpolated themselves as possible witnesses; the proceedings were nearly over, and the verdict about to be pronounced, when after a fumbling at the door Silas Dene appeared suddenly in the room.

He was alone, and in the unfamiliar room he stood stock still, solitary, detached and startling; isolated as a man who has vast spaces around him, regardless of the cheap pitch-pine walls that actually confined him. He was bare-headed, in his working-clothes, as rugged as the bole of a storm-wrecked tree on the borders of a great plain. All gazed at him, and the coroner ceased speaking.

Silas broke the silence to say, in a restrained but threatening voice,—

"Is this the inquest?—I came here by myself," he went on; "I was in the shops. I know Mr. Calthorpe persuaded me not to come. Then I changed my mind. I thought I'd like to hear for myself. Will someone take me to a place?"

They were amazed at his feat of travelling unescorted from the shops where he worked, to the heart of the village, and mysteriously this achievement increased their fear of him, enriching it with a bar of superstition. Calthorpe led him to a central chair, near the coroner, so that he stood in the middle of the room, with his hand on the back of the chair. He would not sit.

"This is very irregular," said the coroner, "I know of no precedent for this, but of course there is no reason why Dene should not attend the rest of the inquest if he wishes. There will be no need for me to call him as a witness now; he attends as a spectator only. Dene, your affidavit was read earlier in the proceedings."

"I want to speak," said Silas.

"If there is anything you want to say, Dene. . ."

Silas stood erect at his full height, ignoring the chair to which he had been led; he had on his most truculent expression. Calthorpe was dismayed, but knew his own impotence. There was a natural force in

Silas that was not to be thwarted. He made other men seem puny; only his brother Gregory matched him, and Gregory was not there.

"I'd like to hear the verdict returned first, if you've reached it," said Silas.

The coroner shrugged his shoulders, annoyed and perplexed, then said,—

"Perhaps that would be as well. With the returning of the verdict the inquest is over, and anything you may like to say afterwards will be in the nature of a private address, not one held in a coroner's court."

He put the usual questions, and a verdict of "Death by Misadventure," was returned, with a rider of sympathy to the widower "in the peculiarly sad circumstances of his bereavement."

"Death by Misadventure," Silas repeated slowly; everybody listened in greedy anticipation; the accident and the inquest both provided succulent material for the curiosity of the vulgar, and to batten upon the exposed passions of a fellow-being—and that fellow-being a Dene!—was an excitement, a treat, albeit an alarming treat, full of surprise and of that quality of danger never very far removed from all manifestations of the Denes. The audience bent forward, with a slight rasping of chair-legs on the wooden floor; they gazed at Silas as though he were an animal at bay, devouring him all the more shamelessly that they knew he could neither see them nor read the unthinking hunger on their faces. He was the centre of mystery and alarm in the village, emerging from his darkness and seclusion only to terrorise. Celebrated as an orator at the village debating society, the men never knew whether to regard him as a leader, an enemy, or an ally. But here his heart, and not his theories, was concerned!

His first words startled them beyond their hopes of gratification,—

"Are you so sure?" He had intoned, but now, seeking effect with the skill of a natural speaker, he dropped his voice a full octave as he swung out into the current of his theme, "It seems to me a paltry sort of thing, to die by misadventure. A paltry ending, to be taken away willy-nilly, like a brat from a party! Why, a man might be leaving many things incompleted, many things he had set his heart on doing before he died. Death by misadventure! I wouldn't set much store by the man that couldn't look after his own life better than that, owning himself the sport when he ought to be the master. It's a shameful thing to be beaten. It's a shameful thing to give up your right of choice. Death by misadventure! a blunder, a clumsy mismanagement, a failure to carry through to the end, that's all."

His audience was amazed at the scorn he contrived to infuse into what was, to them, nothing but a trumped-up thesis. They could not admit that this unexpected, unnecessary, far-fetched thesis could be anything other than trumped-up. Even Silas Dene, full of surprising opinions as he was, could not, with the longest plumb-line, have discovered such an opinion as this anchored in the wells of his heart. He must be joking at their expense—deluding himself, perhaps, in his effort to delude them. A practical joker, Silas; even, it would appear, over his wife's body!

He had paused after his preamble, gathered all his thoughts up into his grip, and began to deal them out to his audience.

"Suicide, now—there's nobility in that. That's grand. That's escape; true escape from a prison. The man who doesn't care a damn for his own life is no prisoner. I call him the contemptuous man. He's a conquerer; he's free. How many of you have got that freedom? and how many have got snivelling, timorous little spirits that cling on to their miserable breath as a treasure? So long as you do that you're bound slaves and prisoners. There's no escape for you.

"You're angry? I shouldn't bait you and gibe at you? Everyone of you is man enough to live up to my principles? Well, the floods are out; they're handy; there's nothing to prevent anyone of you from proving his manhood and his independence. The floods over the fields, and there's the Wash for anybody who'd like something a bit deeper."

He launched this invitation at them with a trivial insolence. "He's mad," they said, and shrugged, crossing their arms in resignation, but they were troubled for all that; he was poking fun at them, a grim kind of fun, and their annoyance increased as they remembered his superiority over them: one couldn't answer Silas Dene, he had read too many books, he returned fire with too many arguments and quotations. He stood there now, apparently ready to go on talking forever, his only difficulty abiding in the variety of his topics, which to choose and which to discard. A little smile played across his lips as he paused, mentally turning over his wares, and surveying the audience which he could not see.

"That's suicide. I see no reason why the man who, so to speak, has always got his finger on the trigger of his revolver and the muzzle of the revolver tapping between his teeth, should fear any pain or hazard. He has his way of escape always open. But there's a braver man than that," he said loudly, "the man who abstains from the death he doesn't fear. Not from religion, not from thoughts of the hereafter; simply from contempt of the easy path. Too proud to avail himself of the remedy he has at hand. All of you who have troubles," he said, pointing his finger at them and letting it range from side to side, sweeping across their rows as they sat, "wouldn't you like to shake off those troubles by the easy way? never to suffer anymore? to leave the responsibility to others?"

They could scarcely believe that a few minutes previously he had been inviting them to cast themselves into the floods.

"I should roar with derision at the man who killed himself to escape his pain," he went on, as though possessed by a demon of mockery, a cold demon that enjoyed goading their bewilderment. Mr. Medhurst frankly thought him diabolic; Calthorpe wondered whether he was in his right mind. "I have the right to speak of it," he exclaimed, suddenly angry; "I spend my life in darkness; let anyone dare to say that I have got no right to speak of pain! I don't complain or ask for pity; I don't want pity, I'll fight against pity so long as I have breath, your pity insults me. But I can speak, because I know death as well as any man who has once stood on the gallows with the rope round his neck and been reprieved at the last moment. I've leant across the border like one leans across a ditch, and touched fingers with death, and then drawn back my hand. You can't say as much. But shall I tell you something?" he added sombrely. "I mistrust myself, whether I have that true freedom; am I truly the contemptuous man? I wonder! but I wonder without very much confidence."

They were impressed, and as he ceased speaking they remained very still; the men thought "Poor devil!" and the women shivered. Calthorpe saw that Nan was straining forward in her place, her breath coming quickly, and her eyes full of tears. As she caught his glance she murmured, "Oh, can no one get him away?" but Calthorpe shook his head, for Silas had already begun to speak again.

III

"That's for suicide, and that's against suicide, and the more you think about it the more you'll be obliged to think about it. Then there's another thing to think about and talk about: murder."

This time his audience was really startled; Nan gave a cry, and Calthorpe saw that she had grown pale, and that deep lines had appeared at either corner of her mouth. He made a movement to go and sit beside her, but at the same time Linnet Morgan shifted into a chair just behind her, and whispered to her over her shoulder, so Calthorpe remained where he was. Mr. Medhurst got up and pointedly left the building. The coroner coughed and said, "Really, Dene, you know. . ."

"I thought you told me, sir," said Silas in his most insolent manner, "that this would cease to be a coroner's court after the verdict had been returned?" The coroner made no answer to this, but began turning over his papers in order to conceal his annoyance, and after waiting a minute Silas continued, "Murder. . . No one will deny that there's as much courage in murder as in suicide. Oh, not in the actual fact, I grant—many of you would say there's no courage, but only a sort of brutal cowardice, in murdering a man unawares, or worse still in murdering a woman,—no courage needed to push a woman under a train!—no, there's no courage in the actual fact, but what about the forethought of it? the first idea, the scheming and the planning, the daily watching of the chosen victim, hey? you must come to a grand pitch of hatred before you can look at warm living limbs and think 'I'll turn you to the cold of death!' Life's great; I've a great respect for life. Life's rich and warm and manifold, and lies outside the bestowal of man. That's why I've so high a regard for life: there's wealth in it, that we can't bestow the same as we can take away. That's why I say there's courage in murder just as there is in suicide,—courage in assuming that liability.

"And consider the afterwards,—the courage in keeping silent afterwards. The man would be living with a secret that took him by the arm as he walked down the street, whispering in his ear, and that snatched bits off his fork at meal-time as he lifted the fork to his mouth,—a playful familiar secret. It'd jolt his elbow at the first sign of forgetfulness. It'd come out with him on Sundays, jaunty. . . He'd know that by a word he could turn his invisible mate into a visible thing for every man to see. The deed wouldn't be finished with the moment the deed was done. Oh no! Crime would be easy enough to the man who had no memory. But memory has long wiry fingers to prod us under the ribs. . .

"Soberly," he continued changing his voice, "let us think: it would be simple for anyone to murder my wife. They could do it in my presence; I'm blind; I should be none the wiser. Let us suppose that, after she left me at the shops that day, someone had seized on her and dragged her away towards the level crossing; she could have held out her arms towards me for rescue, but I should have known nothing—nothing! That's all perfectly plausible. But who should have had a sufficient grudge against my wife? I'm going through the names. . ."

V. SACKVILLE-WEST

A real protest was about to be raised against this hideous entertainment, when a commotion arose:—Nan Dene had fainted.

IV

"Not surprising!" said the woman in commiseration, peering at her where she lay on the floor, "pore little soul!" "Better get her home," said the men, and meanwhile the representative of the directors' board took Silas firmly away from the hall. "Where's Gregory?" asked someone; "At the factory," someone else replied, and Calthorpe, pushing through the throng, said "Here, let me carry her." "Mr. Morgan's got her, sir," said a voice, and Calthorpe saw Morgan rising from his knees with Nan drooping limply in his arms.

Great indignation was expressed against Silas as the factoryhands came in little groups out into the street. In the wan January sunlight Nan was already being hurried away in Morgan's careful clasp towards her own cottage, followed by two women. Silas was on the opposite side of the street, his back against a house, in an attitude of defiance, talking to the director, who looked restrainedly indignant. Silas called out suddenly, pointing with his finger across the street, "Oh, I can hear you whispering! why not say it out loud: Silas Dene ought to be suppressed? but I've been a good friend to you in strikes and troubles, and it's always been, 'Get Silas Dene to speak for us.' . . ."

"Hush, hush, Dene!" said the director; "you're not quite yourself; walk up and down with me for a little." He took Silas by the arm and forced him to walk up and down, talking to him all the time in an earnest and persuasive undertone. The men and women lingered in their groups about the concert-room door, whispering together and watching Silas, but Calthorpe came amongst them and ordered them away. He was peremptory and irritable as they had rarely seen him.

IV

I

THE FOG PERSISTED, TURNING THE world to a strange and muffled place, and seeming by its secrecy to favour the evil deeds of men. Within its shroud a man bent on dark purposes might creep unobserved by his fellow-beings. It could be imagined to breed such purposes, as miasmic places breed fantastic lights and unwholesome growths. It was the more oppressive because it had no tangible weight; only the moral weight, and the obscuring of vision. It was a foul-playing foe, insidious and feline, not to be lifted by strength, or countered by resistance. It was stealthily horrible, as the destroyer of clarity, setting itself mutely but quite implacably against all bright and manifest things, against the proclamation of the sun and the sweet glory of the breeze. Like an influence that intentionally confuses clear thought and strong endeavour, discolouring all that is pure, fostering all that is obscure and fungoid, it made more difficult the road of the traveller, and, waiting ever outside the doors of houses, tried to slip in its unwholesome presence through any crack of door opened to admit it. It wreathed strangely around the corners of houses so entered. The inhabitants of Abbot's Etchery spoke of it as a living thing. "He's terrible thick today," they said, or else, "He's not thinking of going away from us as yet."

II

ON THE HIGHER GROUND BEYOND the marshes the air was clear from fog. Here were knolls surmounted by clumps of beech-wood, the ground beneath the trees rusty with last year's leaves, and the trunks of the beeches themselves bare, lofty, and processional, their clubbed heads shaven against the winter sky. From these knolls one looked down over the brown mirror of the floods, that surrounded the block of the village with the factory and the ancient abbey, and that were crossed until the eye lost it in distance by the great dyke carrying the road and the perspective of stark telegraph poles. But this was only when the fog had lifted. When the fog lay heavy, one looked down upon a white plain of cloud, blackened by a great smear and a fading trail where the smoke of the factory-chimneys rose to mix with it (the chimneys whose summits

V. SACKVILLE-WEST

sometimes reared themselves through the fog like three giant fingers), and concealing beneath it who could tell what stress and labour, what hope or suffering, what secrecy of purpose, what web of mingled and obscurely tending lives?

On the higher ground amongst the beeches stood the big Georgian house belonging to Malleson, a director of the factory and local squire of the district. It was built to turn its back upon the flooded region, and from the front windows and colonnaded façade the view stretched away over the gentle rise and fall of the midland country, the dun fields, clumps of bare trees, grey sky, and cawing rooks,—a landscape in dead and uneventful levels. Malleson was very well satisfied with it. His wife was not. Malleson found satisfaction in the dark tangle of the sleeping hedgerow and the dying brake, and was happy if with gun and spaniel he might wait at the top of a ride for the bolt of a rabbit, or might stand watching woodcutters at their cleavage, and, passing on, come upon a plough-team of his own horses straining across the shoulder of a hill under a wide heaven. He was content to lean over a gate looking across a bean-field, for so long a while that, like some animals, he took on the colour of his surroundings; a hare ran amongst the beans, sat listening upon its haunches, then ran again a little farther; a jay flashed blue between two clumps of hawthorn,—but Malleson, whose interest was professional, and who would never have owned to a more sentimental satisfaction, did not like jays in his woods any better than the presence of hares among his young beans.

Christine Malleson, his wife, hated the country, hated the Midlands, hated Malleson Place, Malleson's spaniel, Malleson's friends, Malleson's relations, clothes, politics, point of view, position in the county, religion, appearance, conversation, and occupations. The only thing she liked about him was his money. In very early days, fifteen years ago, before she knew better, she had given him a son; but in the horror of that one experience,—which had, progressively, infringed upon her comfort, outraged her vanity, terrified her nearly out of her wits in one brief concentrated nightmare, and finally drawn down upon her the irony of Malleson's joy, and of remarks designed to please her, smiling, congratulatory, immemorial, consecrated, fatuous,—all that had taught her never to allow the experiment to be repeated. The months that Malleson obliged her to spend in the country were one long sulky lassitude; she rarely set foot beyond the garden, and in cool weather spent her days in overheated rooms; discontented and fastidious, picking up a book, reading the beginning, and, if that interested her, turning to read the end, but always too languid to read the middle; sleeping on her sofa after luncheon, resting after tea, amusing herself by frequent change of clothes, sometimes staring out of the window while her be-ringed hand held back the muslin curtain, watching for the post that might cheer her by bringing some phrase of flattery or homage, after which event remained only the long empty hours before she found herself, arrived there by some monotonous law of routine, sitting at dinner opposite Malleson.

She never listened to what he said, and indeed when they were alone he spoke very little. She usually leaned her head upon her hand as though she were weary, a head of lovely shape, drooping gracefully; and picked at burnt almonds, or held a cigarette to her lips, for she had a habit that maddened Malleson, of smoking almost throughout a meal. It maddened him, yet he owned that his wife was a very graceful woman, sitting there languid, spoilt, indefinably but flowingly dressed, a woman unlike the wives of other country squires, and within his very scrupulous heart he contested that he preferred her thus, that a woman was designed as an ornament, not for the sturdier business of companionship. He knew that she despised him, and, humble, accepted her estimate, ranging himself low, not putting into the opposite balance the esteem in which men held him. Having long since ceased to think that his conversation might attract her attention, only his loyalty withheld him from admitting to himself that he looked forward to the relief of the moment when she would nod to him and trail out of the room, and he might throw his legs over the arm of his chair with a pipe and a book until he began to reflect it was time for him to go to bed.

III

SHE LISTENED TO HIM, HOWEVER, while he told her about the inquest he had that day attended. She had volunteered an inquiry, and when he said in mild surprise, "My dear, it never occurred to me to mention it, because I know you don't care much for the factory," she replied, "You may as well tell me," thinking how little discrimination he showed between the things that might interest her and those that could not possibly be expected to do so, "Emma said something about it while I was dressing." "Gossip, of course," he said, restrained but displeased, and she shrugged and murmured, "Prig. . ."

In the end he told her, though without enthusiasm; and the story stirred the rather stagnant pool of her curiosity. One or two of his phrases, pronounced meditatively, had put her on the scent of something unusual, something that might while away a portion of the dreary time, though calling for very little effort on her part,—she could not endure the idea of effort. "He speaks like an educated man," her husband had said of the blind factory-hand, "or a great deal better than most educated men speak, and I believe he is entirely self-taught. It appears that he has a hunger for books. . . And a born speaker, like some of those ranting parsons one hears sometimes talking to a crowd from a tub. All the makings of a demagogue. I should like to assist at one of his performances at the debating society; Calthorpe gives me to understand that they're remarkable. He's full of ideas—Utopian mostly—exposes them ably, works them out in both scope and detail, convinces his audience, or at any rate stirs them—and then demolishes the whole fabric—out of pure devilry. I wonder what the fellow's mind is like inside? A black business, I should fancy!"

"I have heard of him before," said Lady Malleson.

"I dare say he is merely a disgruntled Socialist," said Malleson, who was already ashamed of having been led away into such speculative wordiness.

IV

IN THE WASTE OF HOURS, after that, she found her thoughts revolving constantly around her preconception of Silas Dene. At first she smiled indulgently to herself when she encountered that unknown but quite definitely conceived figure, again erect and motionless in the foreground of her mental vision; then she grew resentful of the unknown man who so imposed himself upon her attention, like a grave and persistent apparition, bending upon her his unfaltering gaze. So long as he remained an evocation, she could toy with him; fit theories on to him, like an artist draping a lay figure. She diverted herself greatly by thinking him out at leisure, ordering and re-ordering the procession of her ideas; it was true that she had heard but little about him, yet her theories were clearly formulated: he must be a self-conscious man, humorously so perhaps, (she was not yet certain on the score of his humour, trying whether she liked him best with or without it), but in any case alarmingly so; but whether he had control over the trend of his life, as would seem to be indicated by his raising himself by his own effort above the intellectual level of his class, or the trend of his life over him, she was unable to decide. Was he that being for whom in her discontented, languid, tentative way she always sought,—for in her endlessly renewed hours of idleness she dallied, not unintelligently, with a little practical philosophy,—was he, might he be, that being who lived in perfect consciousness, viewing each incident of life in instant proportion, not condemned to wait for the slow drawing out of years into perspective, but calm, secluded, not so inhuman as to escape the passing ruffle of moods, nor so unreceptive as to escape the stimulus of new influences, but on the whole sternly planned, continuous, progressive, working towards a goal, not drifting towards some end unknown and concealed within the uncertainty of mists? This apprehension, this quality of being aware, was by Christine Malleson so greatly envied, because it was in herself so totally lacking. What did she upon earth? what track would she leave, did she hope to leave? she could not have replied. Would she find in a blind factory-hand that rarest illumination, flung like a straight ray along a dark road,— clearness and wholeness of vision? She knew without being told that he would prove a man of strong opinions; that much might be said of many men, but would he have taken the further step, and welded the scattered material into a system, that could be a weapon of defence or offence, a pix so ably constructed as to appraise the worth of coin both large and small? Was he of that calibre? She thought, potentially yes. She raised her cigarette to her lips, watching the slim blue trail of smoke that rose without wavering in the warm air of the draughtless room. Silas Dene, surely, smoked a pipe, of pungent black tobacco, and along with the specific picture of him ramming in the shreds, she played with the idea of herself as the wife or the mistress of such a man; he would be the experiment in a fine but natural metal, dross and dirt mingled with the gold of the nugget. She allowed herself to drift with the current of this amusement; she was alone, none could read her thoughts, a new luxury was precious to her appetite wearied by ennui, and she had the frankness of acknowledging to herself her craving for any new sensation. She smoked in long inhalations, more concerned with the thought of what she might do to Silas Dene than with the apprehension of what Silas Dene might do to her. She would like to bewilder that man. She would like to test his arrogance, break it if she could. She would like to prove to him that his control of life was based upon no true security. It could not be so based; no poor human could be truly immune. They might think themselves immune until the storm came along. Should she play this experiment, under the guise of Lady Bountiful, on Silas Dene? Should she indulge her curiosity at his expense? The first unseemliness of the idea passed away with surprising ease. He would help her to get through the weary country months. She had tried her hand at most things, this would be something new; something, therefore, amusing. . .

V

I

CALTHORPE CAME OFTEN TO SEE the Denes after the inquest; no one could have been kinder, more considerate, or more attentive than Calthorpe.

No doubt the Denes would have preferred to keep out Calthorpe, as they had kept out everyone else, but he was the overseer, and they tolerated him.

He came on Saturday afternoons, on Sundays, and sometimes on ordinary week-days, during the evening.

He would spend a little time talking to Silas, and then he would knock at Nancy's door and ask her for confidential information.

"Nobody can tell me so well how Silas is getting on as you can, Mrs. Dene," he would say; "may I come in for a minute?" or else "would you stroll down the road?"

Nan never strolled down the road, but she always let him into her kitchen and gave him a chair beside the fire. Sometimes her husband was there, sometimes he was not, but in either case he could not affect the conversation. Nan told Calthorpe one day how it had taken her a little while to become accustomed to the disabilities of the brothers, and to remember that whereas Silas could hear and speak but could not see, Gregory could see but could neither hear nor speak.

"I used to stop and think; now of course I know without thinking. And really you wouldn't believe how one can get on with Gregory: I talk to him with my fingers like I talk to you with my tongue, it's no bother. He's very quick, too, at understanding."

Calthorpe had already noticed that she never lost an opportunity of praising her husband and advertising her own contentment. She was more reticent about her brother-in-law, and when once Calthorpe asked her why, she replied after a slight hesitation.

"Silas can speak for himself; he doesn't need anyone to speak for him."

"He can certainly speak!" said Calthorpe. "Do you remember how he startled us all at the inquest? why, by the time he'd finished, half the folk were wondering whether they shouldn't throw themselves into the floods, and the other half whether they shouldn't go home and strangle their families!"

It was the first time he had directly mentioned the inquest to Nan, and he did so now in full recollection of the effect Silas's speech had had upon her. He had hesitated long over the problem whether he should ever allude to it or no, but recognising the subject as the shadow always in the background of their talks, he had decided to attack it openly, his intent, as usual, kindly.

"It's worried you a good deal, I know," he added.

"Oh," she began,—he knew that little "Oh," by which she prefaced her remarks and which always betrayed her nervousness,—"Oh, I don't think we ought to talk about it, do you?"

"You mean, you don't want to talk about it?"

She got up in a restless way, and busied herself with a vase of wild flowers upon the dresser, turning herself so that her face was hidden from him.

"Mrs. Dene, you don't want to talk about it?"

"Oh, don't *drive* me, please," she murmured, in a voice full of distress.

Calthorpe was very remorseful to feel that he had been the cause of this distress, and he came over to the dresser where she stood arranging the flowers.

"Very well; of course we will never speak of it again," he said, trying to soothe her, but knowing that if his repentance took too affectionate a form she would immediately shy away from him. "What are you doing with those flowers? look, you have upset some of the water! here's my handkerchief to mop it up with."

As she took the handkerchief he saw that there were tears on her cheek, as clear as the drops of water she had spilt from the flowers; but with his large, rough tact he pretended not to notice.

"Where did you find so many flowers, this time of year? Primroses in February! Catkins, of course, and grasses, and a sprig of plum blossom. . ."

"And some wild violets," she said, showing him. "Smell them, how sweet!"

"Well, I wish I had somebody like you to put flowers about my place," he said in a rush of sentiment.

"Will you take these? Yes, please!" crushing them, all wet as they were, into his hands. "I got them in a copse over by Thorpe's Howland last Sunday, I walked over there. . ."

"What, by yourself?"

"No, with Silas and Mr. Morgan; it was Gregory's Sunday on at the factory. We started after dinner, Silas was in a good temper, and I was happy to get away from the floods for a bit. You know, there's a belt of higher ground away there to the south, which never gets flooded. It was nice to see the green again, and to go through woods where the trees didn't stand with their roots soaking and rotting in water. I hate the floods, they're so cruel; cruel in a dull, flat sort of way. . . Gregory likes them; they make him grin. Of course, Silas can't see them, but if he could I'm certain he'd like them too; he's always asking me to tell him just what they're like. But that Sunday he'd forgotten about them. He was as cheerful as could be, repeating poetry all the time as we went along the lanes; he kept stopping and saying 'Now listen to this!' and waving time with his stick as he recited, and Mr. Morgan kept capping what he said, and they laughed a lot, trying to outdo each other." She smiled at the recollection, leaning with her back against the dresser; then Calthorpe saw the smile disappear from her lips as though at another darker remembrance, and the scared look came into her eyes.

"Well?" he prompted.

"Oh. Well, then we went on till we got to Thorpe's Howland, and we made Silas sit under a beech-tree while we looked for primroses. . ."

"You and Linnet Morgan?"

"Yes, I and Mr. Morgan. Silas sat under the tree for a bit, pulling up the moss all round him; then he got up and leant against the tree-trunk, saying more poetry; Shakespeare, I think it was. Mr. Morgan beckoned to me to come and listen, so we crept up on tiptoe, and Silas went on like that for about half an hour; I don't know how he manages to keep it all in his head. I don't like it so much when he starts his poetry in the kitchen, but in the wood it seemed all right; it might have been part of the wood," she said, lowering her voice and hanging her head with her pretty, sudden shyness, and scrutinising her finger nails.

"How do you mean: part of the wood?"

"Well,—there was a lot of patchy sunlight on the ground, coming through the trees, and the moss that Silas had torn up smelt bitter,—like earth,—and the primroses smelt soft and sweet. There was the sort of big sand-pit in the bank, where we had picked them. There were the trees, so gray and naked. There was Silas,—Mr. Morgan whispered to me that Silas looked like a tree himself, a tree that had been blasted by lightning, and when he said that, I saw he was right; even Silas's arms, waving about, were like the branches."

"Well, well!" said Calthorpe, scratching his chin.

"Mr. Morgan's like a son to Silas already," she went on; "he's gay with him, and he's as gentle as a woman. He's never put out by Silas's ways—never seems to notice them, in fact. And Silas likes him because he can talk to him by the hour about all the things he thinks about and reads about."

"But Silas always talks to everybody."

"Yes, he's so greedy for an audience that he'll put up with never getting a sensible answer, sooner than not talk at all. But Mr. Morgan's got education; he'll argue with Silas; he's like a whetstone to a knife. He'll get Silas into a proper excited rage, and then laugh, and Silas takes it in good part. It was a grand day when he came to live in the cottage."

"Yes,—well, I must be going," said Calthorpe, moving away, and he went after a rather sulky goodbye, very unlike his usual friendliness and promises to come again.

II

NAN STOOD STILL, WITH A finger to her lip, after he had gone, then she opened the door and ran quickly after him. He heard her steps, and her voice calling his name and, turning, he saw her, a bright flushed spot on each small cheek-bone, with strands of dark hair blowing across her face.

"Oh, Mr. Calthorpe, I haven't offended you, have I?"

("How tiny she is, and how concerned she looks!" he thought, and nearly laughed with tenderness.)

"Bless me, no, my dear!" he said, patting her arm as one might pat a child's.

"I'm so glad; I was afraid. . . you went away so suddenly. . . You forgot the flowers; here, I've brought them." She held them out, and continued to look anxiously up into his face. "Sure I didn't say anything to offend you—sure?"

"Sure! you're very sweet," he said, taking the flowers.

"You've been so kind; I think you're my best friend," she said impulsively, and she put her hand on his cuff. "I must go back now—but you're not cross, are you?"

"Not a bit; not in the very least."

He walked away shaking his head rather ruefully.

"She won't come for an ordinary stroll with me of an evening, yet she tears after me without a hat or a coat, all upset, for anybody to see! She's got a good heart. . . She's never herself when those Denes are about. But when she's herself she's just as sweet as she can be. Poor little thing! Am

I a fool to go there?" and thinking these thoughts he hurried on, carrying the flowers she had given him.

III

HE CONTINUED, HOWEVER, TO GO there, but he made his visits more rare, reflecting, with a shade of surprise at his own considerateness, that it would be doing her a bad turn to cause gossip in the village. He was, after all, the overseer, while she was only the wife of a factory-hand and a factory-hand herself, so that he could not visit the Denes as another man might, on a footing of equality. The death of Silas's wife had given him an excuse at first for frequenting the double cottage, but that affair was now a month old, and was already beginning to be forgotten in the rude world of the factory-village, where accidents were more or less common. Silas himself never alluded to it. He seemed, as Nan had said, to live in comparative content with Linnet Morgan. Linnet Morgan was young, educated, and extremely clever; and so merry that Silas's dark moods usually ended by being dispelled before his laughter. Linnet Morgan seemed, in fact, to have taken charge of Silas's life.

So much, Calthorpe thought, for Linnet Morgan.

But Nan,—ah! Nan was winning and tantalising, demure sometimes and sometimes impetuous; Nan was shy but confiding; little and sweet and windblown; and Calthorpe tried to feel large and fatherly towards Nan. She evidently welcomed him, gave him his chair by the fire; then went about her occupations, stopping to chatter when she felt inclined, asking him his opinion with her pretty head held on one side and her hands on her hips, singing over her work,—adopting him very much, in fact, as an inmate of her household. This method might put him at his ease, but it also mortified him. She accepted his visits with a lack of self-consciousness, he sometimes thought, that would have been mortifying to any man. He supposed that Gregory was fond of her, but the difficulty of communicating with Gregory rendered too tedious the effort of discovering his thoughts. Calthorpe usually nodded pleasantly to Gregory, and left their acquaintance at that. He thought Gregory a sneering, sour kind of fellow, jealously wrapped up in his machinery; he would not let Calthorpe look at his designs, but covered them over with both hands outspread, when once the overseer bent with a friendly interest over his shoulder.

But Nan,—no, never had Calthorpe blundered across so delectable a being as Nan. He cursed himself for having hitherto overlooked the grace and delicacy which set her so apart from the other working women; he cursed himself anew each time he watched her as she hung muslin curtains across her windows, or arranged and re-arranged her wild flowers upon the dresser. He had to make his observations for himself, for she told him nothing; she did not tell him how she wilted daily as she passed through the factory on her way to her own work, which lay among the heaps of white powder and the myriads of little scent-bottles, and was congenial to her,—soft powder, coloured boxes, gilt labels, pretty cut-glass, and a constant rainbow of ribbons. She snipped them with her scissors, sitting on a high stool before the table, in company with rows of other girls, all in blue overalls; and the ends of ribbon fell in a scatter of confetti around her. She noticed everything that the other girls did not notice. They only lifted their heads to gape at the visitors who were being taken over the factory, but Nan, gentle, uncommenting, and inwardly blandished, dwelt with pleasure upon the bright lightness of the big room, upon the pale sunlight that fell on the bent heads of the girls,—some of them had fair, sleek hair that looked like spun silk in the sun,—upon the powdery cleanliness of the floor, and the scrubbed expanse of the tables between the armies of shining little bottles. She hated the rest of the factory, that smelt and smoked and clanked; but this one room approached her secret vision of diaphaneity and seemliness.

IV

For who amongst men and women lives without the secret vision of some spot, either known or merely conjectural, whether of red moors or sheltered meadows, mirrored coasts or battlemented mountains? Hers was a pitifully simple dream. Sun and water, and always light: light everywhere, streaming and pouring in, because light to her meant happiness. The house must be small, the rooms low; size alarmed her. She would be too timid to dwell beneath vaulted roofs. In her mind she knew its geography intimately, and the disposal of its garden; it stood in the heart of undulating cornlands, not very far from the sea. She had never seen it. And with whom she shared it she did not know. Certainly not with Gregory. Gregory's exclusion was not deliberate; it was unthinking, and, had it been put to her in words, might have perplexed and dismayed her; nevertheless, it was a fact that Gregory's step never sounded upon the tiles of her dream-passage, nor did his belongings lie in the litter of joint-proprietorship about the rooms.

V

INSTEAD OF THIS SHE WAS given flooded, low-lying country, a dark and ancient abbey, and the clanging factory served by fire and iron. She shuddered at the cranes which discharged the coal from the slow canal-barges of the factory's private canal. She compared the barges to beetles, and the cranes that poised above them, to the pincer-armed antennæ of some gigantic spider, descending to devour. When they pivoted slowly with their dangling burdens, she shrank, thinking that the cable must break, either from accident or mischief, and drop the weight upon the men below. She thought the factory would relish that. She never went near the canal wharves or the railway line if she could possibly avoid it, but sometimes she had to take Silas to the "shops"—the packing sheds where he worked, and which were near the railway. He seemed often to ask her to take him there since Hannah had died, and on the way there he would talk about the accident. Nan was unable to answer. She led him conscientiously, holding her black shawl about her head with her free hand, and turning her profile away from him; but though she was careful of his steps she could never force an answer between her lips. No, not if she had known that he would guess his secret had been surprised; nothing could have loosened her response,—yet her terror of him was extreme. She had often to constrain herself from crying out. He walked boldly, really knowing the way without her guidance, and talking in a loud voice, swinging his arms, so that sometimes people stopped to stare at him. He rehearsed and repeated every detail of that day, making a grievance that he had not known of his wife's death until three hours after its occurrence, and Nan shuddered, wondering how he could infuse so much vehemence into a lie. Had he perhaps persuaded himself of its truth? But she little knew the rotations moving in his brain, that dwelt upon the murder as a vindication of his own cunning and courage. That was a deed planned and executed by no bungler and no coward! He delighted fearfully in its elaboration. With every phrase he was risking a slip, as a man walking in a dangerous place risks his limbs with every step. True, he held Nan in contempt, but she did well enough for him to practice on; any suspicion that might raise its head in her mind could easily be laid again by his inventive brain. And after she had left him, he felt flattered and gratified by his own daring.

VI

A COWARD! WAS HE A coward? Surely a blind man had very little choice; deeds of danger were debarred from him, but Silas dwelt amorously upon such deeds—courage pre-eminent amongst the high attributes that fascinated, baffled, and angered him.

By a twist of his brain, through his blindness, courage meant light. Courage shone. It allured him, so that he turned constantly round the image. There was nothing moral about this allurement, it was as pagan as any cult of beauty. Courage moreover—physical courage—carried with it the thought of death, which to his egoism was so supremely and morbidly entrancing. That he should cease to be? . . . he could never adopt this idea. He went up to it, and fingered it, but its clammy touch revolted him, and he violently rejected it always. But he returned to it again and again, working back his way in a roundabout fashion, disguising the phantom under a rich cloak of phrases.

VII

HE WAS SCARCELY MORE WARY in his dealings with Lady Malleson than with Nan, not that he underestimated her intelligence, but because she awoke all his boastfulness, pandered to it, stimulated him as nobody had in the whole of his highly experimental life. The comparative frequency of his interviews with her was kept strictly secret. It was now no longer Nan who led him to Malleson Place, as on the first occasion, but Hambley, whom Silas had terrorised into discretion. Nor did those meetings invariably take place in the house, but sometimes in a summer-house, away from the gossip of the servants, while Hambley was sent to skulk about the park, with orders not to return before an hour, or two hours; and even once, when Sir Robert was in London, Hambley was dismissed until midnight. He offered no objection; the employment was after his own heart, and Lady Malleson, unknown to Silas, made it well worth his while. He knew that he was safe enough over this. When the lady brought Silas to the garden gate, and gave him over to Hambley, Silas could not see what passed between her hand and Hambley's. He could not see Hambley's grin of thanks, or his lifted cap, or Lady Malleson's nod of smiling complicity that enjoined silence. He could only stand by, waiting to be led away, during the little farce that was never neglected:

"Well, goodnight, Dene; so glad you're getting on well."

"Goodnight, my lady; thank you."

"Goodnight, Hambley. Take care of Dene going through the park."

"Yes, my lady; goodnight, my lady."

Then they would turn and go, Hambley leading Silas with care, while Christine Malleson re-locked the garden gate and watched them, always reluctantly, out of sight.

VIII

THAT FIRST OCCASION!

She had long resisted the impulse to send for him. How long? She did not know; everyday had been a week, since the wish first consciously awoke in her. What had deterred her? she did not know that either; perhaps a superstitious shrinking, an instinct that the amusement might turn to a wild beast of danger as soon as she exchanged the tractable wraith of her own evoking for a human creature of independent intentions, of will and muscle. So she had prolonged the period of evasion, knowing perfectly well that at the end of the road she was descending with such restrained, deliberate footsteps, stood the figure of Silas, with folded arms, waiting for her. Sometimes she had wondered whether the whole thing were not the creation of her fancy. The matter had grown in her mind, since she had first heard from her husband the story of the inquest, until the blind man now accompanied every moment of her day; and so strong was this fateful companionship, that she believed Silas, down in the village, must be living in equivalent consciousness of her nearness and the rapid convergence of their lives. Still she attempted to persuade herself that her own idle mind was alone responsible; sometimes with a laugh, sometimes with a shrug, she had tried to dismiss the too persistent figure.

She had not believed her own lips when she heard them giving the order to fetch Silas Dene.

IX

WHEN THEY CAME TO TELL her that he had arrived she had glanced at herself in the mirror, then remembering that he was blind, she thought, "Absurd!"

"Who is with him?" she asked the servant.

"A young woman, my lady."

"Very well; give her some tea in the housekeeper's room. Bring Dene up here."

She lay on her sofa, waiting for him to be brought up. She hoped his blindness was not disfiguring, and suddenly the matter lost its almost mystical value, and she saw it in a prosaic light: why had she been so foolish as to obey her whim and send for this man? she knew that she was very unskilled at talking to what she called "common people," even when she came across them accidentally, such as gardeners; they were always taciturn and hostile, and she thought vaguely that they would be more so within four walls even than in the open air. The prospect of being closeted in her sitting-room alone with a factory-hand,—he was nothing else,—appalled her. Perhaps he would spit. Perhaps he would smell. . . In any case, what should she find to say to him?

He was there, standing by the door where the servant had left him, with the special stillness of the blind in a strange place. Contrary to her expectation, he did not wear a beard. She saw at once that he had an extraordinary proud, fine-featured face, and that his blindness was not in the least disfiguring. Indeed, his eyes were so dark and so full of fire that it was hard to believe them sightless. He had nothing of the smartened-up appearance that she was accustomed to associate with the poor when visiting the rich. He had so clearly taken no trouble either to brush his hair or change his coat, that she remembered with a twinge of annoyance her own glance into the mirror when his arrival was announced. Her embarrassment diminished as she realised that he was himself neither intimidated nor impressed.

"Oh, Dene," she said, "I am glad to see you. Sir Robert has been telling me a little about your circumstances, and I wondered whether I could help you in anyway? So I asked you to come up here to speak to me." She was satisfied with her opening, but felt the last phrase to be weak, a falling away; his quietness, and the knowledge that he could not see her, disconcerted her.

"In what way did you mean exactly, my lady?" he asked.

How could she answer that question? Mention of money was impossible; she knew that already, although she had only heard him pronounce nine words. She was driven up against the truth that she had wanted to see him for no other purpose than her own distraction, that any other reason would be a mere pretext, and she had a swift impulse to tell him this, confident that he would not misunderstand. So much already did she feel him to be not only her social, but also her intellectual equal. (Social was a wrong word, an absurd word; it could never be used, with all the artifice and fallacy that it implied, in connection with Silas Dene. Her discoveries went rapidly. But she must give some sort of answer.)

"I meant nothing exactly. I thought that if there was anything I could do, you would tell me."

"This is the first time, my lady, that I remember your sending for anyone from the factory up to Malleson Place."

She was astonished at that; his tone amounted to an accusation. He was so grave, and she used in her mind the word "chained," as most nearly expressing his obvious reserve of force.

"The truth is," she said, ceasing to lie at full length upon the sofa, and sitting upright, "that I was very much interested in what Sir Robert told me, and thought I would like to see you for myself."

"As your ladyship has seen me now," he suggested, "and there is nothing I want, I can go?"

As soon as he wanted to go, she wanted him to stay. She got up and came to help him, saying, "But I should like to talk to you for a little, Dene; give me your hand and I will take you to a chair."

He shook his head, and said that he preferred to stand. She had to go back to her sofa thwarted, though in so small a thing, while he remained by the door. He made her sitting-room appear tawdry, with its little gilt chairs and lacy cushions and pink carpet, so much did he rob people and objects of all but their true significance. She was almost ashamed of her surroundings, and was thankful that he could not see them, but she thought that it would take more than mere blindness to stay his more perilous vision down through the embellishments into anybody's soul. She was conscious of saying to herself, "This *won't do*," and of taking herself sharply in hand. "This is to be *my* game," she insisted, "not his."

X

SHE HAD FAILED ENTIRELY TO make him sit down, for he continued to refuse her invitation with the same haughty gravity, and responded not at all to the one or two phrases with which she tried him.

"I have heard reports of your fame as a public speaker, Dene," she said with a propitiatory smile, forgetting for the moment that her smiles were wasted on him.

"A lot of the chaps speak, my lady."

"But without your advantages. Sir Robert tells me you are a very highly-educated man."

"No such luck, my lady."

"Oh, come, Dene? Sir Robert says you are a great reader."

"Somebody must ha' been kiddin' Sir Robert, my lady."

She delighted in him. He was perfectly grave, and affected a Lincolnshire accent, which he certainly had not possessed when he first came into the room; a subtle insolence, but one which she did not resent, for it demonstrated him as unwilling to prance out his tricks, cheaply, at the bidding of a sophisticated curiosity, and she was a woman who knew how to esteem superficial, although perhaps not fundamental dignity. (Malleson had fundamental dignity, which, poor man, had not served him to very much purpose with his wife.) Also, she was emphatically a woman who maintained that the first duty of sex in the game was to be a danger to the opposite sex. Dene—certainly Dene fulfilled both these conditions! Acquaintance such as hers with him was like a sojourn at the foot of a volcano which might at any moment erupt. She relished the peril of the game. How she stirred him to extravagance after extravagance! how she poked and probed and decoyed his mind! encouraging, insinuating, blowing upon the ready spark; "baiting Silas Dene," she called it, as a baron might have said, "baiting the bear"; all the better sport because she knew it to be so quick with danger. She sent for him as often as she dared, and when he was absent she thought about him, but always as an experiment, an intellectual exercise. She was too cold-blooded a schemer to allow herself to think of him now as anything else. . .

VI

I

Nan returned frequently along the road on the top of the dyke, on the red and gray February evenings, when the stillness was absolute; on either side of the dyke the floods lay, placid and flat as mirrors, over broad miles of country, reflecting the crimson sun up a path of roughened and reddened splendour. The water-filled ruts along the road glowed with the same light; long narrow lines of fire. How dismal that flooded land would have been without that light; gray, only gray, without the red! All the most dismal elements were present: a few isolated and half-submerged trees stuck up here and there out of the water, and at intervals the upper half of a gate and gate-posts protruded, the entrance to some now invisible field; useless, ridiculous, and woebegone. But that red light, cold and fiery, scored its bar of blood across the gray lagoons.

The village lay in front of her, at the end of the road, and behind the village rose the three high chimneys of the factory, black amongst the gray waters, the gray sky, threatening and desolate in the midst of desolation. The three black plumes of smoke drifted upwards, converged into a large leisurely volume, and dispersed; already in the dusk the red glow at their base was becoming visible, and a single star appeared high above them, as though a spark that had floated out from the heart of the factory now hung suspended in supercilious vigil. The abbey on the farther side lay heaped in a mass as dark as the mass of the factory. Nan would shift to the other hand the basket she was carrying home from the market-town of Spalding; walking along the elevation of the dyke, she made a tiny, upright figure in the great circle of the flat country, for here the disc of the horizon was as apparent as it is at sea. The group of village, factory, and church, emerged like an island loaded with strange and sombre piles of architecture, adrift from all other encampments of men. Abbot's Etchery lay before her, against that formidable foundry of the heavens, that swarthy splendour of smoke and sunset, and as she continued to advance she thought that she re-entered an angry prison, too barbarous, too inimical, for her to dwell beneath it, and live.

II

THE CALM, COLD WEATHER BROKE late in February; a gale swept for two nights and a day across the country, beating up the waters into little jostling peaks and breaking from the forlorn trees branches that were jerked hither and thither upon the waves, now coming to rest upon a tussock of higher ground, now taken again by the shallow storm of the floods, or tossed to lie against the bulwark of the dykes. The smoke from the factory chimneys was snatched by the wind, and swirled wildly away in coils and streamers, black smoke mingled with the dark masses of cloud that drove across the disordered sky. Gulls from the Wash flew inland,—the gulls, that more than any other bird attune themselves to the season, in summer gleaming white, lovely and marbled, on the wing, but in times of tempest matching the clouds, iron-gray, the most desolate of birds.

It became unsafe for carts to travel along the road on the top of the dyke, since one farm-cart, swaying already under an excessive load of fodder, was caught by a gust of wind and overturned. After one moment of perilous balance, it crashed down the embankment, dragging after it the two frenzied horses, falling in a welter of broken limbs, tangled harness, and splintered woodwork, while the trusses of hay broke from their lashings and scattered into the borders of the flood.

The storm of wind and water raged round this disaster, and folk from the village collected on the top of the dyke to gape down at the carter busy amongst the wreckage, and surreptitiously at Malleson, the owner, who stood alone, more in sorrow for his valiant horses than in regret over his material loss. There was no hope of saving the horses,— they were shire horses, stately and monumental,—by the time the crowd had assembled their tragic struggle had already ceased. The carter was sullenly bending down, unbuckling the harness; he would speak to no one. On the top of the dyke the gale buffeted the little crowd, so that the men (their hands buried in their pockets, their overcoats blown against their legs as they stood with their backs to the winds, and their mufflers streaming) stamped their feet to keep themselves warm, and the women with pinched faces drew their black shawls more closely round their heads and whispered dolefully together.

III

THE ACCIDENT GREATLY EXCITED SILAS Dene; it occurred on a Saturday afternoon, and Nan, who was sewing in her own kitchen, heard upon the wall the three thumps that were Silas's usual summons. She found him with Linnet Morgan, Hambley, and Donnithorne, one of his mates, who had stopped on his way down the street to bring the news.

Silas wanted Nan to go to the scene of the accident and to bring him back a first-hand report. She cried out in dismay, appealing with her eyes to both Morgan and Donnithorne. Hambley she ignored; his very presence made her shudder, and she knew he would side with Silas.

"But, Silas, I wouldn't for the world! Those poor horses—what are you asking me to do? to go and gloat over them?"

"Sentiment!" said Silas, who was angry. "Linnet says the same. God, if I had eyes to use. . . There's violence and destruction half a mile down the road, and you won't go to see it. It maddens me, the way you folk neglect the gifts and the opportunities God offers you. Sentimentalists! A fine rough smash-up. . . the wind's a poet. A poet, I say, wasting food and life for the mischief of it. The food of beasts, and the life of beasts; wasted! There's twenty trusses of hay in the floods, so Donnithorne here tells me,—twenty trusses spoilt for dainty-feeding cows,—and two fine horses smashed, and a big wagon. They're lying heaped at the bottom of the dyke. There's blood spilt, as red as the heat of the sun. No man would dare to bring all that about for the sake of the mischief; but the wind's a poet, I say—I like the wind—he tears up in a minute trees that have persevered inch by inch for a thousand years, and sends to the bottom ships full of a merchant's careful cargo. Well, you won't go down the road and tell a blind man about the smash?"

"Guts spilt, Mrs. Dene!" said Hambley, rubbing his hands together and provoking her. She turned away from him with repulsion.

"Ye're morbid, Silas," said Donnithorne in disgust, his hand on the latch. He was a red-headed, red-bearded man, with pale but lascivious blue eyes that once had leered at Hannah, Silas's wife.

"Morbid, am I? no, it's you squeamish ones that are morbid, and I that have the stout fancy. If Heaven had given me eyes! I wouldn't be such a one as you. I'd sooner be a fool playing with a bit of string, and crooning mumble-jumble, or taking off my hat to a scarecrow in the dusk."

With that he bundled them all out, and slammed the door.

IV

Linnet Morgan followed Nan back into her own kitchen.

"Oh, Mr. Morgan, is Silas mad?" she said, turning to him at once.

"I sometimes don't know what to make of him."

"Would he go to look at the accident, do you think, if he could see?"

"Not he!" said Morgan, "not he! But he's safe to say so. He turned pale when Donnithorne told him about it, but next minute he was pretending to be all eager, like you heard him."

They remained standing, occupied with their own thoughts. Gregory glanced up from his drawings as they came in, but otherwise took no notice of them. Morgan sat down before the range, and began prodding a piece of firewood between the small open bars.

"I lose my bearings, living with Silas," he said presently; "amongst all his manias, he's got this mania for destruction. Perhaps the long and short of it is, that he likes talking loud about big noisy things, when he's certain they won't come near him to hurt him. Being blind keeps him safe. . . Mrs. Dene, come for a turn with me. You look right white and scared. Come out, and let the wind blow away bad thoughts?"

"I'll ask Gregory to come with us." She went over to her husband, touched him on the arm to attract his attention, and spoke to him on her fingers. "He says he's busy with his drawings, but will we go without him."

V

They took the road that led in the opposite direction from the accident, and uncharitable eyes watched them go past the windows of the houses in the village. But they walked all unconscious, feeling relieved and with a gay sense of holiday, almost a sense of truancy; and when the wind caught them as they left the shelter of the village, and forced them to a breathless standstill, they laughed, and struggled on again, exhilarated by their fight against so clean and natural a foe. They were soon in the open country, having left the village behind; they breasted the wind, and breathed it deeply, tasting, or fancying that they tasted, upon their lips the salt of the flying spray. The road which they followed lost the monotony of its straightness when they conquered it yard by yard, and remembered that, did they but follow it far enough, it would lead them eventually to the sea.

There was indeed a regal splendour about the day, about the embattled sky and driven clouds. The northern forces had been recklessly unleashed. The sea would be beaten into a tumult full of angry majesty. How wild a day, how arrogant a storm!

VI

Coming back, the wind almost forced them into a run, and they yielded, racing along the road, impelled as by a strong hand. They could not speak to one another in the midst of the turmoil, but they smiled from time to time in happy understanding. As they neared the village Nan checked herself, and, leaning breathless against one of the telegraph-posts that bordered the road, tried to re-order her hair, but the wind took her shawl and blew it streaming from her hand, also the strands of her hair in little wild fluttering pennons. Nevertheless, she was in such high good humour that she only laughed at what might have been an annoyance, turning herself this way and that to gain the best advantage over the wind. Morgan stood by, laughing himself, and watching her. She wore a dark red shirt, and the wind had blown two patches on to her cheeks, which were usually so pale they looked fragile and transparent. They continued more soberly towards the village, still without speaking, even when they reached the shelter of the street, because it seemed unnecessary.

They saw Silas standing on his own doorstep, hatless, in a strange attitude, holding his hands stretched out before him, the fingers wide apart. Nan ran up and caught one of his hands; Morgan was surprised, for she never treated Silas with levity. She seemed to have shaken off the years of repression, to have forgotten totally the conscientious lesson.

"What are you doing standing there, Silas?" She was very gay.

"Letting the wind whistle in my fingers. Hark! Bend down your head."

"I can't hear it, Silas."

"No, you've coarse ears; eyes! eyes! yes! but coarse ears. Where have you been?"

"Along the dyke. . ."

"Seen the accident?"

"Hush, Silas; you shan't dwell on that." Morgan had never seen her so brave, so radiant, with the blind man. She took his arm now, leading him back into his cottage. "Sit down by the fire, Silas; it's warm and sheltered in here. The kettle's singing."

"I'd sooner stay in the wind," he said, striving against the light pressure of her hands on his shoulders as she held him down.

"The wind's too rough; I've had enough of it."

"Then let me stay on the doorstep alone. You stop in the shelter with Linnet."

"No, Silas, we'll all three stop in here together. I'll sing to you a bit, shall I?" Morgan observed her firmness with a surprised admiration.

She got her zither from the cupboard where she kept it, laid it on the table, and tried the chords with a little tortoiseshell clip that she slipped over her thumb. The thin notes quivered through the bluster of the wind and the harshness of Silas's voice. She bent intently over her tuning, trying the notes with her voice, adjusting the wires with the key she held between her fingers.

"Now!" she said, looking up and smiling.

She sang her little sentimental songs, "Annie Laurie," and "My boy Jo," her voice as clear and natural as the accompaniment was painstaking. She struck the wires bravely with her tortoiseshell clip. Morgan applauded.

"It's grand, Mrs. Dene."

"Why do you choose today for your zither?" Silas asked in his most rasping tone.

"It's Sunday, Silas,—a home day."

"But you're not home; you're in my cottage; your home is with Gregory, next door. You're here with me and Linnet."

"Gregory can't hear me sing," she said pitifully.

"Then why don't you dance? he could see you dance."

"I asked him to come for a walk," she said, her brightness dimmed by tears.

"And he wouldn't go? with you and Linnet?"

"No, he was drawing."

"Ah?" said Silas. "But Linnet went with you? Linnet wasn't busy?"

"What'll I sing that pleases you?" she said, maintaining her endeavour; "'Loch Lomond?' You used to like 'Loch Lomond.'"

"Ask Linnet; he's Scotch; no doubt that's what put a Scotch song into your mind."

"Silas!" she said in despair, dropping her hands on to her zither, which gave forth a jangle of sounds.

"If you want home, as you say, stop here with Linnet; I'll lend you my cottage," said Silas, rising and groping for his cap. "Play at home for a bit. Draw the curtains, light the lamp, make tea for yourselves, put the kettle back to sing on the hob, and you, Nan, sing to your zither to your heart's content. It's a pleasant, warm room, for pleasant, warm people. Home of a Sunday, with the wind shut out! Oh yes, I'll lend you my cottage. Gregory's lost in his drawings till supper-time. Stay here and talk and smoke and sing, while the room grows warmer, and you forget the wind and the two dead horses and spoilt fodder lying down the road. Spend your evenings in forgetfulness. Ask no questions of sorrow. Kill darkness with your little candle of content."

"You're crazy; where are you going?" cried Morgan.

"Only to the Abbey,—not into the floods," Silas replied with a laugh.

"To the Abbey? alone?"

"One of my haunts, you know."

VII

SILAS FOUND HIS WAY ALONG the village street by following the outer edge of the pavement with his stick; as he went he snorted and muttered. "I'll have nothing to do with Nan's kindness," he said to himself several times. "She's easily satisfied; she's comfortable; she's grateful. She shuts the eyes that she might see with." This thought made him very angry, and he strode recklessly along, knocking against the few folk that were abroad on that inclement evening. One or two of them stopped him with a "Why, Dene! give you a hand on your way anywhere?" but he rejected them, as he was determined to reject all comfort and patience that Nan might offer him. He liked the wind, that opposed him and made his progress difficult; he struck out against it, the struggle deluding him into a reassuring illusion of his own courage. He welcomed the wind for the sake of that tortuous flattery. . .

He would have made his way to Lady Malleson, but he was afraid to venture under the trees in the park, where a bough might be blown down upon him.

VIII

AT THE END OF A side-street the Norman abbey rose, black and humped and semi-ruined, the huge dark clouds of the evening sky sailing swiftly past the ogive of its broken arches. The village had retreated from the abbey, because the abbey's furthermost walls were lapped by the floods, so that it remained, the outer bulwark of man's encampment upon the inviolate mound in the midst of the inundations; it remained like some great dark derelict vessel, half beached upon dry land, half straining still towards the waters. The street which led to it was a survival of the ancient town, gabled and narrow, with cobbled ground; Silas tapped his way over the cobbles. He could not see the enormous mass of tower and buttress and great doorway, that blocked the end of the street before him, but he heard the scattered peal of bells, and the deep gloom of the abbey lost nothing in passing through the enchantment of his blind fancy. He entered, and was swallowed up in shadows. The roof was lost in a sombre and indistinguishable vault. The aisles became dim colonnades, stretching away into uncertain distance. The pillars with their bulk and gravity of naked stone dwarfed the worshippers that rustled around their base. The organ rumbled in the transept. Silas moved among the aisles, handing himself on from pillar to pillar; he imagined that he moved in a forest, touching his way from tree-trunk to tree-trunk; he conceived the abbey as illimitable, and relished it the more because ruin had impaired the intention of the architecture.

The organ from its rumbling broke out into its full volume, a giant treading in wrath through the forest, a storm rolling among the echoes of the hills. Night came, and the clouds moved invisibly past overhead, over the abbey and the floods. Nothing but the dark flats of water lay between the abbey and the sea; its bells gave their music to the wind, and the great voice of its organ was more than a man-made thing. The black shape of the abbey on the edge of the desolate floods bulked like a natural growth rooted in old centuries, harmonious and consonant with nature. To the vision of Silas Dene, on which no human limitations were imposed, and whose mind was fed on sound and thought alone, the abbey was not less vast than night itself, only a night within the night, an abode of ordered sound within the gale of sound. In his fancy he was not clear as to whether it were roofed over, or lay open to the sky; he could vary his decision according to the vagary of the moment, alternately picturing the rafters high above his head, or the scudding moonlit heavens of ragged black and silver. He put his hands upon the pillars with no thought of man's construction; they seemed monolithic. He caressed them, moving between them, leaning against them, and listening to the organ. He was in a large, dim, mysterious place, that had a kindred with the floods and with the storm. He knew that all around him were shadows which, while making no difference to the perpetual shadow he himself lived in, obscured and hampered the free coming and going of other men. Darkness was to him a confederate and an affinity; he would smile when people spoke of nightfall or of an impenetrable fog. He searched now with his hand until it touched the shoulder of a kneeling woman.

"Are there any lights in the church?" he whispered.

"Why, surely!" she said, startled, "candles upon the altar."

He was displeased; he moved behind a column where he knew the shadows would be deeper. The organ had ceased, and he heard prayers. He shook with inward mockery, confident that the abbey, which he had endowed with a personality and had adopted into his own alliance, would reject the prayers as contemptuously as he himself rejected them. It would await the renewed majesty of the organ. . . To Silas the organ represented no hymn of praise; it represented only the accompaniment of storm; he was not even troubled, because he did not notice them, by the infantile words which the congregation fitted to its chords. It had never occurred to him to think of the abbey as a holy temple until he came by chance upon a thing to which his imagination made a kindled and ravenous response.

For once he had not made for himself the discovery of this new theme in the course of his reading. He owed it, a resented debt, to the conversation of his mates in the shops. Silas, listening, had felt his ever-ready contempt surging within him; it angered him to learn from illiterate men of a subject that he alone amongst them was fitted to understand. They skirted round it; but he grasped it avidly, adopting it, as though a niche in his mind had been always waiting for it. He took it with him to the abbey, like a man carrying something secret and deadly under his cloak. Black Mass. . .

He scarcely knew what it meant. He took it principally as a symbol of distortion and mockery. It seemed to be one of the phrases and summings up he had always been searching for, he who liked to condense a large vague district of imaginings into a final phrase.

When he remembered Black Mass in the ordinary way, he smiled in satisfaction, and stowed it away as a secret; but when he thought of it in the abbey he hunched himself as though he were in the throes of some physical pleasure. In bringing that thought with him into the abbey he was taunting a tremendous God, a revengeful God; and he exalted fearfully in the latent implication of his own daring. Surely courage could go no further than the defiance of God! His ready ecstasy swept

V. SACKVILLE-WEST

him away. The world he lived in was a reversed world, where darkness held the place of light; in the world of his soul a similar order should prevail. Taut-strung, he cast around for some piece of blasphemy, some monstrous thing that he could do,—he did not know what. He only knew that now he was brave, though it might be with the courage of hysteria; presently he would be again afraid. He dreaded the return of his cowardice. He had not been a coward the day he had killed Hannah; only afterwards; he must not dwell upon the afterwards.

He had no weapon with him in the church except his voice, and a penknife in his pocket.

He must achieve something; something! anything!

In the midst of his excitement he took it into his head that a piece of the ruined masonry, detached by the wind, might fall in upon him and crush him. Still chattering under his breath to himself, his hands nervously working, he moved closer to the shelter of the pillar. Here he felt more secure, but still the gusts of storm sent waves of physical anxiety through him. He was torn between that small anxiety and the illimitable defiance.

The organ swelled out again, lifting him upon its great rhythm as a wave lifts a swimmer.

VII

I

I<small>T WAS ON THE SAME</small> unpropitious evening that Silas's only son returned to his home from Canada.

The train discharging him at Spalding, he fought his way against wind and rain, along the lonely road on the top of the dyke. He trudged with his hands in his pockets and a bundle on his back, the peculiar bleakness of the road returning familiarly to him after his absence of seven years. It was dark, but through occasional rifts the moon appeared, showing him the floods; they were familiar too,—their wide flat stretches lying on either side of the high dyke, and swept by the East Anglian wind straight from the North Sea,—he knew in his very bones the shape and sensation of the Fens; this was homecoming. There was a knowledge, a grasp of the size, shape, and colour—almost of taste and smell—a consciousness that marked off home from any other place.

When he reached the village, he felt in similar manner the presence of the factory on the one hand, and of the abbey on the other, with the village lying between them. His boots rang on the stone of the pavements. That was the school, and this the concert-room. . . He reached the double cottage of his father and his uncle; he thought he would surprise his father and mother, so without knocking he turned the door-handle and went in.

Nan was still sitting by the table on which her zither lay; her hands were clasped and drooped listlessly. Her whole attitude betrayed her dejection. Morgan stood by the range talking. They were alone, and young Dene recoiled, thinking he had broken in upon strangers, though the smile was still broadly upon his face, with which he had prepared to greet his parents' surprise.

"I've made a mistake," he muttered, "this used to be Silas Dene's cottage. . . my name's Martin Dene."

He was a bronzed young man, with thick black hair, a Roman nose, and a fine curved mouth; a proud face, like the face upon a coin.

"Can you tell me where my father lives now?" he added. He looked at them frankly; he took them for a young married couple.

"Why, Martin!" cried Nan, recognising him.

"Why, it's Nancy Holden," he said almost at the same moment. They greeted one another gladly. "You're married? living here?" he asked, with a glance at Morgan.

"Married to your uncle Gregory. . ."

"No! He could be your father!" exclaimed young Dene naïvely, and again he glanced at Morgan.

"Oh, no," said Nan, flushing, and she hurried on with an explanation, "Your father lives here still, but he went out a little time back; he said he was going to the abbey. He'll be in presently. Sit down; I'll get you a cup of tea."

"But where's mother?" asked Martin Dene, and in his impulsive, attractive manner he strode across the room, flung open the door that led to the staircase, and shouted "Mother!"

II

"What's that?" cried Silas, startling them all.

They had not heard him come in. He stood on the threshold, his hand outstretched, the likeness between himself and his son strongly apparent. "What's that?" he repeated; "who's that, calling 'Mother' here?"

"Silas, it's Martin come home," said Nan, who was trembling and who had gone, quite unwittingly, closer to Morgan.

"Martin? it's suited him to come back, after seven years?" Silas uttered a derisive "Ho!" He added, "It's too late, my boy, to come here calling 'Mother.' That's rich, that is—eh, Nan?"

"What d'you mean?" said Martin Dene, swinging round.

"Your mother's dead, that's what I mean."

"Dead?"

"Yes, dead three months ago."

"Dead! Mother dead? why? how?"

"Tell him, Nan."

"Look here," said Morgan, speaking for the first time, "I'm sorry you've got to learn this news. . ."

"Oh, smooth it over! water it down! I didn't know you were there, Linnet," interrupted Silas. "I'll tell him myself. Your mother was killed in an accident—picked up unrecognisable—run over by a train—now you know. Got anything to say?"

"My God!" said young Dene, covering his face. Nan went up to him and began to whisper to him; he heard her half through with horribly staring gaze, but then, disregarding her, he cried in a hoarse voice to his father, "Accident be damned! you drove her to it. I know your ways—they drove me away to Canada, and Elsie to London—I've seen her there—and they drove mother to *that*—come, own up! it was suicide, wasn't it?" He made a movement towards his father, but Nan clung to his arm.

"No, I swear it wasn't," replied Silas, full of a grim amusement at his suggestion.

"Well, how did it happen, then? What's your account of what happened? Did anyone see?"

As neither of the others answered, Morgan said, "Nobody saw it happen."

Martin leapt on to that. "So it was never explained?"

"No," said Morgan, "the coroner's inquest gave Accidental Death." Martin laughed.

"You're going now, I suppose?" said Silas, "Morgan's answered you, and his answer can hardly satisfy you. Suspicion's a sleepless guest in the mind."

"You're alone now, father?" asked the son. His tone altered as a sort of pity and repentance overcame him, and as he remembered his father's blindness. "Perhaps I spoke too hasty, father; see here, I'll stop on with you if you like."

"I don't like; you can get out," said Silas. Morgan and Nan gave an exclamation.

"I'll stop tonight; we're not calm, either of us."

"I don't remember you calm, somehow?" Silas sneered. Martin's temper, which he had controlled, rose again.

"I'll get out, then," he said, moving towards the door. Nan, through her terror, thought him very handsome,—bronze and black, his bony cheeks still glistening from the rain.

"You needn't bother to come back, after another seven years."

"Don't you worry, father; I won't come back."

"Martin!" cried Nan. This flare of quarrel between father and son troubled her greatly; it was a disturbance of harmony, and she longed for the re-establishment of peace, at the same time dreading further questionings, further possible accusations; Martin would probe and examine, Silas might lose his head,—Nan, knowing the truth, lived in the perpetual terror of a frenzied outburst of candour on Silas's part. . . He was, she knew, quite capable of such an outburst. Life, and the harmony of life, would be less endangered with Martin out of the way.

But this was an unkind greeting for Martin at his home—poor Martin! after seven years' absence and a trudge in the rain, to find his mother dead and his father ferocious!—Nan's fund of pity overflowed, and she tried to compromise: "Martin! you can't walk back to Spalding through this awful night; stop till tomorrow with Gregory, and me."

"Not he!" said Silas, unexpectedly, and as though he spoke with pride.

"You're right, father,—though I thank you, Nan; you mean it kindly."

"They mean everything kindly, Martin," said Silas, indicating the other two. He continued to speak with the same curious understanding towards his son. Nan and Morgan, separately, stood repudiated and estranged.

Martin Dene nodded, his eyes meditatively upon them.

"Won't you stop, Martin?" urged Nan's timid voice.

"I've said an unforgivable thing to father," he said, turning to her, in patient explanation.

"But you didn't think it, Martin; tell your father you didn't think it."

"I did think it; I still think it; father knows that. I shall always think it. That's why I can't stop. So long," he said, shouldering his bundle; he nodded to them again and went out.

III

"ARE YOU SATISFIED NOW, SILAS, are you satisfied?" Silas kept mumbling to himself later as with haste he tore his clothes off in the dark.

He would tell Lady Malleson—tell her that he had wantonly thrown out his own son. What would she think of that? Once she had said he was terrible; he hoped that she would say it again. The words had crowned him with a rare reward. Surely he had earned their repetition?

He scrambled into his bed; lay there with his muscles jerking. He tautened them, trying to keep them still, but could not. Martin, yes; he had thrown out Martin. That was a resolute thing to do. It was all of a piece with what had gone before; Hannah had ministered to his comfort; in a rough and ready way, it was true, often more rough than ready; but still she had ministered; and Hannah, along with his personal comfort and convenience, had been sacrificed when necessity dictated. (If he chose to consider in the light of a necessity the suspicion of an outrage upon his own sensitive dignity which another man might have dismissed as negligible, even inevitable, that was his own business; nobody else's.) Hannah had gone. Now Hannah's son, for a quick, intuitive suspicion of his father, had gone too—thrown out to founder, possibly, though the sequel was now no concern of Silas's; Martin was proud, Martin would not return, least of all to appeal for help. Lying awake in the night that to him was no more deeply night than midday, Silas fought his regret for Martin. Martin had come, his memory rich with what garnered tales of peril? he had led a hunter's life among red men, bony, painted, feathered men; he had tracked wounded beasts, either great-horned or soft-footed; he had dared the great solitudes, blazed his way through forests, and taken his chance of the rapids; with all this, Martin, a fine young man, would have beguiled his father's ears and opened new horizons to his insatiable fancy. Bringing all this with him, like a pedlar's pack, Martin had tramped along the dyke from Spalding; no doubt with a certain pitiful eagerness he made his way home from the incredible distance of that rough primitive world. Tears forced themselves out from Silas's sightless eyes. He had never wept for Hannah, he had hated Hannah, even when through her death she became, poor woman, an object of satisfaction to his insecure vanity; an object, too, of allurement to his prowling cowardice. But for Martin he wept, for Martin and all that Martin stood for. Then envy shook him, that Martin, free, young, keen-sighted, and, above all, fearless,—fearlessness was the only true freedom,—should be returning to that worthy life, in more ways than one a hunter of big game. Big game! to the simple, eager nature all life was big game. The actual quarry; the stake in a hazardous enterprise; the test of endurance; or the interlude of women,—all that was big game; a big, audacious, masculine game. The hint, the mere passing suggestion, of enterprise acted as a sufficient stimulant, under which his imagination flamed at once as a torch, widening a bright, lit space in the darkness, populating it with figures full of splendour, heroically proportioned. He reached out to another and more ardent life, away from the security in which he so carefully preserved himself. He was pierced through by the sheer valour of man, as a shaft of light might on a sudden have pierced his darkness. He beheld man, small, imperfect, but dauntless; sustained by a spirit of extraordinary intrepidity, intent upon the double mastery of his planet and of his own soul; man, stern against his own weakness, checked here and thwarted there by the inner treachery of his own heart, foiled in his ambitions, cast down from such summits as he had attained, but ever fighting forward in the pursuit of an end perhaps undistinguishable, to which the path of conquest, so difficult, so jeopardous, was in itself a measure of recompense. So he was blind, as blind as Silas himself; the more honourable because, despite his blindness, he still wrought undeterred.

How various were his pursuits, his methods of conquest! to maintain and advance himself in the supreme captaincy; so diverse the images of vigour which the labourer in his activity was too simple to suspect. There were men who wrested from the earth the last guarded secrets, pitting their limbs against forest, mountain, ice, or waterless plain; only their soft limbs against the giant sentries of unhandseled nature; those who scored the monotonous sea with the rich and coloured roads of commerce, heaping in the harbours of the world the strangeness of cargoes, always strange because always exotic; those who tilled the responsive soil; the hunters, the fighters, and the princes; others who, living their true life, sequestered and apart by reason of their austere calling, through a patience so immense that the profound darkness of the mysteries with which it dealt was punctuated by reward of fresh light only here and there along the wide-spaced generations, gained fragment by fragment the knowledge of the ordering of distant worlds; the women who bore the burden of fresh lives,—he could feel himself alien to none of these, neither to the law-givers nor the law-breakers; the acquiescent nor the rebellious; no, nor the spare anchorite who aspired through lonely frugality and penance towards the same summit of domination; he stretched out his hand, alike to king and prostitute, and with the falling strove still to uplift the tattered standard, and with the multitude of the triumphant marched upon the road of pride. All this he saw with a clarity, a wholeness that was in the nature of actual beholding far more than of the blurred confusion of a vision. He had his landscape under sharp sunlight, precision of detail allying itself with breadth of horizon. He saw, too, skulking in and out amongst the pageantry rich with legend that went its way under windy banners, he saw dark, puny, ignoble figures; not one of them bore the tool of an honest craft, but small forked tongues darted between their lips; and in his abasement he included himself in their number, and questioned whether the rest of them, damned spirits, worshipped in secret, as he did, the magnificence they must envenom because they could not share?

IV

THEN WITH A RUSH OF incredulous disgust the constituents of his own existence stood out in the same white light; confused, craven, petty;

a tangle that he despised and loathed with a weak fury, the more that he could not extricate himself. Envy without emulation, spite without hatred, violence without strength! Then the personages: Hambley, the lick-spittle go-between; Christine Malleson, whose pretended mental companionship with him disguised the claw of cruelty; inanimate objects, the floods, the gale; Hannah, a ghost now, not a personage, a ghost that gave him no rest, try as he would to weld the whole incident to his own uses, to the furtherance of his own self-confidence; Martin, sacrificed for the same purpose; Nan, the object of an as yet ill-defined, floating malevolence that crouched ready for a spring on to the back of the first poor pretext; all the men, his fellows, in whom he amused himself by fostering dissatisfaction; and, lastly, he found that he must include an animal in this lamentable population,—the donkey on the green, that, no less than the others, had, that evening, fallen a victim to his need for mischief; the coarse pelt was still vivid under his fingers, as he had slid his hand down the leg, till he came to the fetlock, and he remembered now the sharp puncture of the knife into the sinew, and the animal's start of pain—to this, to this had he sunk! when he crept out from the abbey, his soul seething with blasphemy, and his fingers closing over the penknife in his pocket! A small, mad deed,—all that his soul in travail could bring forth. In this deed, tinily terrible, had his exaltation culminated; the exaltation engendered by storm, by the disaster on the dyke, by the organ swelling in the ruined abbey, by the suggestion of the Black Mass.

He rolled from side to side in his bed, tearing at the blankets with his teeth.

He directed his despair and fury then against Christine Malleson, making her responsible for this ruthless savagery which always possessed him, without system or goal beyond a need to damage everything that was happy, prosperous, and entire. True, she was partly responsible; she was responsible for the pranks of experiment that she played upon him, stirring and poking his mind, his ambitions, into a blaze, and the chill "Don't forget yourself," with which she quenched the flame. He raged against Christine: she had him at a disadvantage; he must strive always to compete with her serenity of class; she drew him out from his own class, aroused his angry socialism, laughed at the gaps in his knowledge, gave him glimpses of a life whose significance and habit he could never encompass, but which he burnt with an envious hatred to destroy; then she would laugh at him again,—she, who had come down from her heights to walk curiously in his valleys,—she would laugh, and he would fling away into fresh magniloquence, seeking to impress her; and when the time came for him to take his leave, the excitable irritation provoked by her remained still unappeased, consuming his vitals. But this he believed she did not suspect. So far as he knew, he had deceived her; he had passed off upon her the old fraud of making her believe him strong when he was, in reality, the bewildered, unhappy prey of his own weakness. The thought that he had so deceived her gave him a little satisfaction. He would tell her about Martin; she would catch her breath. He would not tell her about the donkey. And he swayed again from the paltry tangle of his own life to the bright heroic visions that alone contented him, weeping with an incurable sorrow, but whether for Martin or the vague grandeur of the unattainable, he could not well have said.

VIII

I

IF THE FLOODS WOULD BUT retreat! If the winter would but dissolve and allow spring to break over the land! Then the rich black loam of the fields would appear in the place of the water,—that flat and cruel, unprofitable water,—and the country under the blush of green would cease to be so mournful, rayless, and forbidding. The floods were so dead; dead brown, dead level; there was no life in them, except sometimes under the red sun, a fierce, angry sort of life, and sometimes when the wind beat them; but now gray rainy day succeeded gray rainy day, mild indeed, but not spring, not the spring of clear sunlit showers and rainbows! It would be a dark, fertile country that came to light, curiously un-English in its effect of unboundaried acreage, wide ditches marking off the fields in the place of hedges. Ditches and dykes would remain as the scar and testimony of the floods, the dykes that like some Roman aqueduct stretched away into the flat and misty distances.

Yearly Nan lived through the winter in the hope of such a spring, and almost yearly it failed her. She was drawn towards spring with an instinct of unsatisfied youth. It appeared to her like a vista cut in the darkness of the life she led between Silas and Gregory.

The population of her world was so restricted; in very early days she had been sharply taught that Gregory would neither welcome his wife's friends at his fireside, nor allow her to go to theirs. She had never forgotten the written message he had left for her on the table in the first week of their marriage, having found her laughing in the kitchen with another girl: "No *prying eyes* here, missis." The Denes, she learnt, were as sensitive as they were savage and solitary, and, so strong was the legend that they had created around themselves, that she had found herself quickly alienated from the rest of the village and definitely regarded as of the company inhabiting the lonely cottage. Silas, Gregory, Linnet Morgan, Donnithorne sometimes, Mr. Calthorpe. That was all. The two dominating figures were Silas and Gregory; she was more frightened of Silas than of Gregory, because of her secret knowledge, but Gregory was like a stranger to her; she was submissive to him but felt no nearness, no intimacy; he was more closely allied to Silas than to her. Of Linnet Morgan she thought with shy and oddly pleasurable evasion.

Of Calthorpe, with confidence; she liked his well-brushed hair, precisely parted down one side, and the close pointed beard that gave him a certain robust dignity and rather the appearance of a sailor; thinking of Calthorpe was like leaning up against a solid and stable building. He looked at her with great kindliness now, when she talked to him; she had always wanted somebody to look at her like that. It awoke, too, in her a certain pride: she had trained this big man in the part she wanted him to play; she, so small, had taught him, so large, a trick, and whenever she brought him her confidences, and he responded with that look so full of kindliness, he was doing the trick she had trained him, against his will, to do. This gave her a proprietary sense in him. She found him very docile. He, on his part, loved her for her little domineering manner.

It was only when she returned to Silas and Gregory that she was made to realise her own futility. Against the weak pushing of her hands they remained immovable. . .

Then she fell sometimes into despair, and her courage crumpled. For days she would be silent, then with an effort she would bring out her zither and sing, until before their contempt her voice would trail away again miserably into silence.

She longed for the retreat of the floods and the end of the winter, because now the country and the year seemed to be conspiring with Silas and Gregory.

II

ONCE SHE TRIED TO BRING about a complete revolution in all their lives; only once. She was really half-crazy with despair when she made the attempt; nothing else could have given her the courage. As it was, she was intimidated by her own audacity, for by nature she accepted circumstances without questioning. Inaugurations terrified her; yet here was she, Nan, inaugurating.

She sat at the table, under the lamp, Silas and Gregory on either side of her, the remains of supper before them. She sat twisting her hands; swallowing hard.

She began, "Shall we be here always?" then stopped, then plunged on again, "living always here, with the floods every winter, all the winter through? Why shouldn't we go away, somewhere else, if we choose? Why shouldn't we?" she cried suddenly, in a frightened voice, as nobody answered.

She looked at Silas and Gregory; Silas was smiling, and Gregory was smiling too, in a twisty, derisive way, as though he knew what she had been talking about. Yet he couldn't know. Silas had a look of surprise and amusement; grateful surprise, as though she had provided him with an unexpected amusement in an hour of boredom.

"Go on!" he said to her.

At that she felt all her source of boldness, of inventiveness, dried up within her. What was the good of this struggle for escape when she was hemmed in, not only by the floods and the dykes, but by those two immovable men who owned her? But her terror urged against her hopelessness; and was the stronger.

"Can you *like* living here?" she appealed to Silas, trying to touch him upon his own inclinations.

"As well here as anywhere else," he answered. "I work here."

She knew the bitterness that edged his voice whenever he mentioned his work.

"You tie up parcels in a packing-shed," she said, "always the same,—work that a half-wit could do. Yes, a poor wanting creature could do your work. Why don't you bestir yourself? Why don't you come away?" She talked so, knowing that she strained to pull a weight that lay solid against her small strength.

If only Silas or Gregory would get up, she thought that with that insignificant display of mobility her hope would revive; but they sat on either side of her, cast in bronze. If they were doomed men, then they made no effort to escape their doom. Too proud, perhaps. They sat and waited. They seemed too indifferent to care.

"Nobody's put you in prison into Abbot's Etchery," she murmured.

Yet they were so like prisoners, Silas in his darkness, Gregory in his silence, that she almost looked for gyves about their wrists and ankles. When they stirred, it should have been to the accompaniment of a heavy clank. When Silas fought, when he cried aloud, it was the struggle of a chained man. But his struggles were so ineffective; Nan, who was not oppressed from within, but only from without, thought that he could help himself if he would. She had all the impatience of the naturally buoyant with the dogged tragedy of the fatalistic.

"Come away," she urged. "What is it that keeps you here? There are warm, pretty places. Let's make the best of things."

"I might get away from Abbot's Etchery, I shouldn't be getting away from myself," said Silas.

V. SACKVILLE-WEST

Nan cried out, "*Can't* one get away? Who says so? Isn't it in our own hands?"

"Is it?" replied Silas, letting drop the sorrowful query as though it were rather the echo of a perpetual self-communion revolving in his soul, than an idle response.

The old mournfulness, the old anguish, closed down upon them again. They were like haunted people, who would not help themselves. They seemed haunted by the past,—which contained indeed the death of Hannah, a death so rough and dingy,—by the present, and by the overcharged future. But their dread was not to be defined; it was of the nature of a mystic sentence, presaged from a long way off. Sometimes she thought that they were afraid of themselves; sometimes that they were too apathetic to be afraid. Only Silas made his dungeon clamorous sometimes with his wild revolt, that led to nothing, to no change, to no illumination.

III

CALTHORPE FOUND HER SITTING LISTLESS in a corner. She showed a hunted preference for corners, and for shelter behind furniture.

"Why, you're pale," he said. He came closer, "You're wan."

She did a rare thing: she put her hand into his and let him hold it, which he did as though it were a child's. He was overcome by her smallness and frailty; she seemed to be almost transparent, and her features were tiny and delicate, but her eyes were large as she raised them. "Not ill?" he asked. "No," she replied, "only tired and afraid."

"Afraid of what?"

"No, not afraid really; only worn."

"Yes, indeed; you're like a little wraith. You'd blow away in a puff."

He could not rouse her at all; she made no complaint, but sat very quiet and beaten, letting her hand lie in his. In reply to his questions, she kept on saying that she was tired. He knew that she meant spiritually, not physically, tired. She was very polite to him, saying "No, thank you, Mr. Calthorpe," and he found her extremely pitiable, but his science failed him when he tried to think of a remedy. He could only sit alternately patting and pressing her hand. She gave him a grateful smile, at length.

"You do me good, just by being there."

"Come, that's better; won't you tell me now what was the matter?"

"I only want to be happy," she said suddenly, and her mouth quivered beyond her control, so she bit her under-lip and looked away.

"Oh, my dear! my dear!" said poor Calthorpe.

"I want to run by the sea, over the sands," she cried, as though her heart had burst its compressing bonds; "I used to live by the sea once, in the south, and I think about it. . . and the birds nesting. There were gulls upon all the rocks. There were white splashes down the rocks. It wasn't home. But I'm homesick, I think."

"You're just a child," said Calthorpe. "You want to play. Poor little soul!"

"Oh, how kind you are," she said, and he felt her fingers flutter within his hand. "I get so tired of fighting, sometimes. . ."

"Won't you tell me just exactly what you're fighting against?" He was very patient and full of pity, but believing her to be slightly hysterical he had the reasonable man's reliance on a calm statement of her difficulties to disperse much of their bogie-mist.

She only said, however, "I don't know."

("Hysteria," he thought. If she had said, "Forces of darkness," he would have started mistrustfully, without allowing himself to be impressed. But she was too ignorant to use the phrase.)

"Come, then," he said heartily, "it can't be a very serious enemy if you can't give it a name,—what?"

"It's everything," she said, "the floods,—I hate them,—the factory. . . If the factory would stop, sometimes, but it never does: always that black smoke, and the men working in shifts to keep it going, and then the men always talking about wages, and sometimes the strikes. Even the abbey gets to be like the factory."

"You're fanciful," said Calthorpe.

"Anybody would get fanciful, living with Silas and Gregory," she replied mournfully.

How she changed! he reflected. Sometimes she ordered him about, and sometimes she came to him like a child for consolation. Whatever her mood, he never ventured upon familiarity. He told himself sometimes with irritation that he had never been kept so at arm's length by an otherwise friendly woman. He was a wholesome and masculine man, and he had a wholesome and masculine liking for the company of woman in his hours of relaxation, and in regard to Nan had certainly intended their friendship to run upon different lines, harmless enough, but perhaps a little more stimulating; he found, however, that quite quietly it was she who decided the direction, while he in aggrieved but unprotesting surprise fell meekly in with her wishes. He often told himself that he was wasting his time, and would go no more to the Denes' cottage, but he always broke his resolution.

"Is Morgan no help to you? he's something young about the house."

"I don't speak to him much, he's always in his books. I wish you lived in the house, Mr. Calthorpe."

"I wish I did, Nan." But on the whole, he thought, he was glad he didn't.

IV

MORGAN, WHOM NAN REPRESENTED AS being always in his books, was by inclination a scientist, but for the moment, until he had the means to devote himself to his profession, he managed that branch of the factory concerned with scents and powders.

He worked among shining alembics and great-bellied bottles of dark green glass, standing round his room in rows.

The latticed window was hung with cobwebs. The table was littered with bottles, saucepans, test-tubes, and little flames burning. Of all things in the room, the alembics alone were kept clean, gleaming bright brass globes, pair by pair, connected by twisting pipes, and ever dripping the distilled, overpowering scent into dishes put ready to receive it. They shone out from the disorder of the room. Canisters ranged round the walls on shelves: benzoin, civet, frankincense, ambergris,—the names on the labels smouldered as a group of Asiatics among ordinary people.

Nan was sent up with a message to him in this room.

She appeared in the doorway, continuing to knock as she pushed open the door, in the bright blue overall she wore when at her work. She was smiling shyly, as though she expected a welcome. But he did not immediately see her. He was bending with great absorption over a little pair of scales, weighing a quantity of grains, and when he had done this he poured the grains very carefully into a kind of box, which he set above a small lamp to heat. Then as he wiped his hands on a piece of linen, he caught sight of her.

"Mrs. Dene! What brings you here? what bit of luck? What extraordinary bit of luck?"

He went to her, drew her into the room, and shut the door. He gazed at her with incredulous delight. He wanted to touch her, to make sure that she was real.

"Why don't you tell me?" he queried, as she stood there smiling but not speaking.

As she delivered her message, every word seemed to give birth to an unspoken, irrelevant flight of words that fluttered round them with ghostly rustle of wings, finding no resting-place. When she had finished, she stood irresolute.

"I must go back."

Her eyes roamed over the room, and every now and then swept over him in passing. They caressed him in that quick, diffident, gentle way she had. They rested with a mild dismay on all his disorder, and a pucker of trouble appeared between her brows.

"What's the matter, Mrs. Dene?"

"Oh, your things want straightening," she murmured in tones of distress. "Doesn't anyone have charge of your room? The dust,—look at it! The litter!"

She moved to his table as though her deft hands were yearning towards it. She made little tentative touches at his things, while he watched her. She looked at him to see whether she was annoying him.

"Oh, do you mind?"

"On the contrary, I like to see you doing it."

She gained courage.

"You haven't a duster, have you?"

He discovered a duster in the table drawer and gave it to her; like all good workmen, she was heartened by the touch of an instrument, however humble, of her natural work. She picked things up and set them down more briskly, saying meanwhile, half in excuse for her briskness,—

"I must hurry, or they'll be missing me downstairs."

"You can say I kept you. I'll find something for you to take to the forewoman; that'll be an excuse."

"An excuse—is that right, do you think? But your room *is* in a mess, isn't it? It can't have been touched for months. Does no one clean up?"

"No, I won't let them."

"You ought to have told me," she said, greatly distressed. "I am so sorry. . . I didn't think. Some men are like that, I know. They think they can find things better. But I haven't tidied; look, nothing has been moved."

"I told you I liked to see you doing it."

"You were civil," she said, not comforted.

"No, I'm never civil."

"Oh yes, Mr. Morgan; you can't help it, if you're civil in your heart. It comes kindly, to folk who laugh as much as you do."

"You laugh too; I've heard you laughing downstairs, in the workroom. You and I laugh more than Silas and Gregory."

"Gregory can't laugh," she said gravely.

For a moment their chatter stopped quite short. Then she began again,—

"I must go now, Mr. Morgan."

"No, stay; you shall look at some of my things," he cried, making a movement to detain her. "These are the alembics where the scent is distilled," he went on; "of course, these are only the small ones that I use for my own experiments; I expect you've seen the big ones in the shed downstairs.

"The shed all littered with sandal-wood shavings? I like it; it smells good."

"It smells good here in my room too, don't you think? That's because of the scent dripping from the alembics. You see it drips into these pannikins that are put there to catch it. They are all new scents—new combinations of scents, that is—that I'm trying." He was eager, both for the sake of his work and in his anxiety to hold her interest. "Now I'll show you some of the raw material; it doesn't always smell good before we've been to work upon it."

He wondered whether he might take her arm, whether he might venture. She was like the little bird to which he always compared her, and as easily scared! He turned the question over and over in his mind while he was talking, now bracing himself to be bold, now shrinking back; almost moving towards her; but while hesitation still swirled within his mind he found that his hand had, quite simply, taken hers. "It's so natural, so fitting, for me to take her hand, that she hasn't even noticed," he thought with joy.

"These are the canisters where I keep my raw stuff," he said, pointing to the tin canisters ranged on shelves. They stood hand in hand reading the names on the labels.

"Ambergris—that's the name of a scent I bottle," she said, with a little laugh. "I use a lavender ribbon for that. And orris—that's the powder. Don't they have queer names? Opoponax, that always makes me laugh."

They laughed together over opoponax.

"And there's names out of Scripture," she said, "frankincense and myrrh."

He took down the tin of benzoin, and made her smell it, shaking some of the brittle stuff into the palm of her hand; crumbling up her hand into a cup, and guiding it now to her nose and now to his own. They compared their tastes; "I think this sort smells nicest," she said to him, gravely holding out her cupped hand, but he would not agree, after bending over it with the deliberation of a practised critic, and added a little storax, which, he said, brought out the pungency of the benzoin.

"All these gums and resins," he said, "come from trees; you cut a gash in the tree, and the gum comes from it like blood from a wound, oozing out. And one of them—labdanum—is got by the natives by beating the bush with long whips; or sometimes they get it by combing the beards of the goats which have been browsing off the bush."

That made her laugh too, but she was impressed by his knowledge, and that made him laugh in his turn.

"Now I'll show you the woods,—you said you liked the sandal-wood; well; this is cedar, don't you like that even better? Shall I give you some to take away in a little packet? you can keep it with your clothes, like the sachets you tie up downstairs." He thought with a momentary panic that he might have offended her by referring to her clothes, but the hint of intimacy in the suggestion pleased and troubled him so much that he was glad he had taken the risk for the sake of that pleasure.

She was not offended; she only blushed a little.

"That will be nice,—but I'm taking all your time, Mr. Morgan."

"Oh no; I have plenty of time, and there's lots more that I could show you. I could tell you a good deal, too, that might amuse you: how the Egyptians used to embalm their mummies, and how an Assyrian king caused himself to be burnt with all his wives on a high pyre of scented boughs sooner than fall into the hands of an enemy. And how the Chinese hunt for musk; this is musk; it doesn't smell nice in this state, but it's very precious. This is attar of roses in this little bottle; smell very carefully. Let me hold it for you. Do you like my things?"

She liked his things very much.

"Do you think my room less untidy and dusty, now that you know there are other things in it besides dust and untidiness?"

"All those tins, full of sweet scents," she said unexpectedly. "Only, I ought to go back to my work now, don't you think? You said you would give me something to take to the forewoman."

"But you said that wasn't right."

"No, perhaps it isn't,—Oh, I see: you're teasing me. Well, I'll go without it."

V. SACKVILLE-WEST

"But you're frightened of being scolded?" he said, following her and laying his hand upon the handle of the door. "Now aren't you? confess! What do you say when the forewoman is cross? Do you stand hanging your head and twisting your apron?" He was laughing down at her.

"She isn't often cross, but she will be if I stay dawdling here,—oh, *please*, Mr. Morgan!"

He saw with astonishment that her eyes were suddenly brimming with tears, and her soft mouth quivered.

"You are dreadfully unkind, getting me into trouble and then teasing me about it," she said, nearly crying, but trying to conceal it from him. "I enjoyed looking at the scents, and I forgot the time, but now it is all different, and I want to go away, please. Please take your hand off the door-handle," she continued, trying to pull away his fingers with her weak ones.

"Why, you have got quite excited," he said gently; "look, I am not keeping you—I have let go of the handle—but won't you wait while I write a note to the forewoman? I want to send her a message, I really do! Won't you wait for it?"

"Of course, if you ask me as one of the girls, I must."

"You're terribly perverse!" he exclaimed, half annoyed.

"If you ask me as one of the girls. . ."

"Very well; Nan, will you please wait a minute while I write a note for you to take to Miss Dawson?" He was not sure to what extent she was serious or joking. Then she flushed at his use of her name, but he saw that she was not joking at all. "What a strange, perplexing thing!" he commented inwardly, as he searched for a pencil among the litter on his table.

"If you're looking for your pencil, I put it in the tray with your measure and the little thermometer," she volunteered sulkily.

It was on the tip of his tongue to say, "You said you hadn't tidied!" but a glance at her face, which was still quivering with her aroused sensitiveness, warned him not to tease her. He sat down and wrote his note while she waited over by the door, then he brought it across to her.

"Have we quarrelled?" he said wistfully.

"Is there no message with the note?"

"How severe you are!" He held the note just out of her reach, risking her anger if he might keep her a moment longer. "Have you got the packet of cedar-dust I gave you?"

"Yes."

"Where?"

She made one of the patch-pockets on her overall gape, and let him see the packet within. He gave her the note reluctantly, and opened the door for her.

"Goodbye, Mr. Necromancer, with your alembics," she said.

"Stop! where did you get that big word?"

"Out of a book."

He could think of nothing to say but "What book?" in order to delay her, but she was already half-way down the passage. He watched her till she was out of sight, then returned to his room and shut the door. "She's like a little delicate moth flitting through gross life," he thought, and he wandered about his room, touching the things which had taken her fancy most.

IX

I

He was on duty at the factory that night, so Silas, not to be alone, had his supper with Nan and Gregory. The households of the double-cottage were so interchangeable that it increased Nan's sense of restriction within that grim and tiny circle, the monotony of knowing that after supper Gregory would bring out his roll of drawings and flatten them out on the table with drawing-pins, and that Silas would surround himself with his great Braille volumes, running his fingers over the pages while his eyes would remain fixed on some distant corner and expressions of amusement, interest, or indignation uncannily succeeded each other upon his face. To watch him while he was reading never ceased to fascinate and frighten Nan. To see him laughing when no one could tell what he was laughing at, when his eyes were not even bent upon the page!

But tonight she had other thoughts. They were not thoughts, they were a timorous, shying riot, that took hands; danced; and upon detection broke up into a scattered rabble. She knew only that they were lovely, and felt the soft muslin of their garments as they passed her. Not thoughts! no, they were more like wings, song, and breeze all chasing one another in her heart. Even the bronze presence of Silas and Gregory could not weigh against their feathery loveliness. She was bewildered, turning this way and that with hands outstretched, trying to capture one, to hold it, and examine it; but she could not, either because it eluded her, or because she feared to rub away its bloom and colour. She was like a girl, blindfolded, playing blindman's buff in the midst of a ring of children. She sat quite idle, not consciously thinking, not even conscious that she was happy. For the moment she was completely happy; she had forgotten both Silas and Gregory. Calthorpe would not have found her wan; her cheeks were flushed and her lips parted, but so abstracted was she that she did not know it. She did not know that she was idle, although she was usually busy over some little industry. She had lost all sense save that of well-being and deliverance.

II

Silas recalled her as he shut his volume with a bang.

"What are you doing, Nan?"

"Oh. . ." She rebelled against this inquisition, irritated for once because she was startled. For all that she lived between a blind man and a deaf one, she had perpetually the sensation of being both watched and overheard. Her instinct leaped to a pang of guilt in being detected idle, and she resented the unspoken criticism. "Nothing, Silas; thinking."

"What about?"

"I wondered what you were reading," she lied.

He reopened the book, always eager to share out his own impressions. Trying page after page with his fingers, he came at last to the passage he sought. She saw the raised letters standing up in their strange shapes, casting strange little shadows.

"I'll read to you, shall I?"

He began to read,—

"How fair is thy love, my sister, my spouse! how much better is thy love than wine! and the smell of thy ointments than all spices!

"Thy lips, O my spouse, drop as the honeycomb: honey and milk are under thy tongue; and the smell of thy garments is like the smell of Lebanon.

"A garden enclosed is my sister, my spouse; a spring shut up, a fountain sealed.

"Thy plants are an orchard of pomegranates, with pleasant fruits; camphire, with spikenard.

"Spikenard and saffron; calamus and cinnamon, with all trees of frankincense; myrrh and aloes, with all the chief spices.

"A fountain of gardens, a well of living waters and streams from Lebanon.

"Awake, O north wind; and come, thou south; blow upon my garden, that the spices thereof may flow out. Let my beloved come into his garden, and eat his pleasant fruits."

Nan was not able to speak; she had listened with indrawn breath, and her hand had flown upwards to her heart.

"I don't like that—sugar!" said Silas resentfully. "You liked it, I expect? This suits me better,—

"I will even appoint over you terror, consumption, and the burning ague, that shall consume the eyes and cause sorrow of heart: and ye shall sow your seed in vain, for your enemies shall eat it.

"And I will set my face against you, and ye shall be slain before your enemies: they that hate you shall reign over you; and ye shall flee when none pursueth you.

"And I will break the pride of your power; and I will make your heaven as iron, and your earth as brass:

"And your strength shall be spent in vain; for your land shall not yield her increase, neither shall the trees of the land yield their fruits.

"I will also send wild beasts among you, which shall rob you of your children, and destroy your cattle, and make you few in number; and your highways shall be desolate. . .

"And upon them that are left alive of you, I will send a faintness into their hearts in the lands of their enemies; and the sound of a shaken leaf shall chase them; and they shall flee, as fleeing from a sword; and they shall fall when none pursueth."

Nan had not listened; the music of that other verse was running in her drunken head, "Spikenard and saffron; calamus and cinnamon; myrrh and aloes, with all the chief spices. . ."

"Half of the Bible should be printed in blood," said Silas, meditating the fulminations, "and read with a spear in the hand.—But it's a trick, a trick!" he said, instantly checking his enthusiasm, with the mocking twist on his mouth, "I do the trick myself, sometimes, to demolish it," and turning over the pages of Leviticus, he came across a sheet covered with his own handwriting, which he gave to Nan. "Read it aloud."

She read,—

"Consider how miserable a pigmy is man, who for his most terrible fancy conceives bulk, weight, and uproar; the magnifying of what he commonly beholds.

"Get hence, thou starveling, thou poverty-stricken of spirit! let thy poor eyes dictate; creation was not given unto thee.

"God said: I will be niggardly toward my servant; the earth will I give him, and the sea and the sky shall be his; but in his heart shall he find no separate image.

"Look, then, within thy heart: what shalt thou find? a perishable hate, a faltering resolve, and, for thy richest treasure, the swift feet of love.

"Terror shalt thou find, and care; the terror of the seen and the unseen; of the steps that pursue thee, and the voices that cry out thy name.

"These shall be thy companions; that shall clog thy spirit throughout all thy days."

"Well? hey? shorn of its magic?"

"Oh, Silas, to laugh at the Bible and write such bitter things!"

Silas roared with laughter; he clapped his hand upon his knee.

"You little fool. Shall I redeem myself? Give me a pencil and paper."

She gave it to him in a dream. "A garden enclosed is my sister, my spouse; a spring shut up, a fountain sealed. . ."

Silas was writing; he wrote and chuckled, and handed the sheet to Nan.

"Then man turned and said: 'All these things are true.'

"But look again within my heart; thou shalt find charity there, and pity like a healing ointment; reverence before strength, and courage as an archangel in bright armour.

"Blow but upon the embers of truth which thou shalt find, and they shall leap as a flame; truly, thou shalt re-kindle the spark of thy breath in man.

"So shalt thou not say in anger, 'This man which I have made is nothing worth.'"

"Does that please you better?"

"It's surely not right, Silas."

"Right! a fig for right and its insipidity!"

("Insipid!" her heart rebelled; what could be insipid when light was over the whole of life? new light, young light?)

"That first bit you read. . ." she began, "it reminded me of the scents at the factory; it was funny your reading just that bit."

Silas said nothing; he was biting his nails and muttering; she resumed, drawn onward though reluctant.

"It put me in mind of Mr. Morgan's room; he has things like that—spikenard and saffron, and the rest."

"Morgan's room—how do you know?"

She was terrified by his pounce upon her out of the heart of his abstraction.

"Oh, I was sent there with a message."

"Today?"

"Yes, this afternoon." Although she was guiltless she had all the quick panic of guilt,—what should she say? what must she not say? hold concealed?—and she felt that Silas held her pinned down beneath talons while he pried.

"What message?"

"Miss Dawson wanted something."

"What did she want?"

"To know whether he had ordered some printed labels." Again that panic of guilt, reassured now because she could answer his question without stumbling. She almost wanted to call his attention to it, to say, "Look, I'm telling the truth; there's no necessity for me to invent."

"So you went up to his room?"

"Yes."

"And you saw the spices?"

"Yes—I was just saying, wasn't I? that it was funny you should choose that bit to read aloud."

"I expect he showed them to you—he's always talking about them to me—did he?"

"One or two—yes, he did show me. But I couldn't stop. I had my work waiting." She regretted ardently that she had introduced the subject; she not only feared and mistrusted Silas's inquisition, but she also shrank, as with physical pain, at his handling of it. He was rough and defamatory.

His tone changed, and unexpectedly he continued in a gentle, interested, and sympathetic voice.

"I'm glad to think you make friends with Linnet. I often think it's hard for you, living between me and Gregory; you're a young thing, so's Linnet; it's natural you should be drawn together. He's got a brain, too; none of your young fools! I've a grand opinion of him. I thought when he first came to the house that you and he would get laughing together. Tell me what he looks like?"

"What he looks like, Silas?"

"Yes, describe him to me."

"He has short curly hair and always laughing eyes."

"Anything else?"

"Oh, he looks younger than his age."

"How old would you think him?"

"Oh, about twenty-two, twenty-three."

"How old are you, Nan?"

"Twenty-one."

"And he's twenty-five. It sounds good. I'm fifty. What more about Linnet?"

"I haven't looked at him so closely, Silas."

"You mean you haven't noticed anything more?"

"No, nothing more." She had no shame, but rather pride, in the lie.

"If I had eyes, I should make better use of them," said Silas, not disagreeably. He went on, "I've helped you and Linnet, haven't I? sent you for walks together, left you alone in my kitchen more than once? I'm less soured than you think me. I'm sorry for you sometimes, being young, and I liked helping you to Linnet as a playfellow. You reckon on me, little Nan."

She did not know what to make of this. She wanted to believe that Silas meant to be kind; indeed, in spite of her latent scepticism she was touched; but she was alarmed by and resisted the insinuations of his words, which he had spoken in a lower voice, as though in an unnecessary precaution of secrecy before Gregory; she glanced at Gregory, poising his beautifully sharpened pencil over his drawing, and his fine looks, and coarse rough hair, appeared to her distasteful. She looked at Silas, so similar in build and feature, yet with a certain slyness that was wholly absent from his brother. Silas was speaking again,—

"If you need anything, come to me, little Nan. You're good to me, and it's not forgotten. We'll be allies."

This was the kind of phrase that frightened her, and whirled her away before she was well aware, to a region of tacit admissions and implications. Had she said more than she meant? more than she even thought? Why, she thought nothing, or had thought nothing until Silas began, but now her sense of undefined well-being was taking shape, emerging from the mist of rustle and cadence, as the coast-line of undiscovered country emerges from the sea mists of dawn. She had been rushed; Silas had rushed her. She thought with terror of how Silas had fastened upon her first words; one could believe that he had only been waiting for her to pronounce them. He had been so ready. He had fired so many questions. He had obliged her to say, or at least to admit, by her silence, anything he wanted. He might not want much yet, but later? later?

Apparently he was satisfied for the moment, for he picked up his Braille volume and fell to running his finger tips over the pages, smiling to himself.

X

I

SHE HOPED THAT THE SUBJECT would be forgotten. It was not forgotten. That was clear to her, although Silas made no direct allusion; but by his manner he established the existence of a secret between them, and because she dared not say to him, "There is no secret," the secret remained, growing insidiously. She was nervous and uneasy in his presence. Silas was kinder than ever she had known him, kinder and gentler, also he appeared to be more contented, but she had a terrified suspicion that he was contented only because his mind was occupied, and it seemed horrible to her that she should be the centre of that occupation. She had suddenly become involved in an affair whose existence, she protested to herself, had its being solely as the outcome of Silas's imagination. She tried to shake it off and to laugh it away, but he held her to it. She had the helpless sensation of being on the end of a rope that he was slowly hauling in, maintaining his purchase over every miserly inch as he gained it.

Hambley, soft-footed, insinuating, and urbane, added by his parasitic presence to the uneasiness of the house. The yellow faced, thin little man, with his black hair and his long front teeth like a rodent's, never had an opinion of his own, but echoed Silas, or cackled with the laughter of approval. He alternately tried to provoke and to propitiate Nan and Morgan, gibed at them when they were civil to him, and fawned on them when they were curt. Nan shuddered when she wondered how many of Silas's darker thoughts were shared out to his keeping.

Was there a conspiracy against her? To her mind, full of alarm, this seemed not impossible. Calthorpe even,—her prop, her kind, comfortable friend,—Calthorpe mentioned casually, "I may have to steal Gregory from you, my dear; I must have a man with me when I go to Birmingham to look over some new plants, and I fancy that your Gregory would relish the job, and be very useful to me." She had clasped his arm. "Oh no, don't take Gregory away, Mr. Calthorpe." "What!" he said in surprise, "are you so fond of him?" She did not answer. She was not fond of Gregory; he was an owner and an institution, but the question of fondness played no part. Hitherto, she had not thought of disliking him; that was all. He and Silas (until she knew Silas was a murderer) had appeared very much the same in her mind, the only difference being that whereas Gregory had rights over her passive and uninquiring person Silas had none.

"Well, am I not to take him?" asked Calthorpe.

"Yes, take him," she replied. Why had she hesitated? By all these doubts and hesitations she was playing Silas's game; he had gained another inch of the rope. "When are you going?"

"It's all quite uncertain; I may not be going at all. But if I go, it will be sometime next month, and I shall ask for Gregory. I am discovering that he has the real knack for any kind of engine; he's sulky about it and contemptuous, but I urge him, and he unfolds. He showed me some of his plans—but you're in the clouds?"

II

SILAS WAS WITH LADY MALLESON, more than usually morose. She lay upon the sofa, while he prowled up and down the room.

"Dene, you scarcely speak to me today?"

("She cringes," he thought with pride.)

"My sister-in-law's in love," he replied tersely.

"With whom has she fallen in love?" asked Lady Malleson, thinking how strange it was that she should be thus intimately conversant with a group of work-people down in the village.

"With Morgan,—the young zany."

"Why, you always seemed so fond of him! your one human frailty," she bantered. But he rounded on her with unwarrantable sharpness. "I think your ladyship is mistaken: I never remember saying I was fond of Morgan. They're neither of them anymore alive than a turtle-dove sunning itself in a wicker cage."

"You strange creature—have you *no* natural affections?" she said, with indolent curiosity. "None for that young man, who really devotes himself to you? none for your little harmless sister-in-law?"

"I'm nothing to them—only a blind man to whom they're kind out of their charity."

"I don't believe, Silas, that you are so bleak as you make out."

"My own solitude, my lady, is my own choosing."

"Why shouldn't you accept what comfort those two young things could give you?"

"It's weak," he burst out, "why not stand alone? why depend on another? Why shouldn't the strength of one suffice? Why all this need to double it? Love's wholly a question of weakness; the weaker you are, the more desperately you love. A prop. . . Love's the first tie for an independent man to rid himself of. It's a weakness that grows too easily out of all proportion. I want my mind for other things, not for anything so trite. So well charted. So. . . so recurrent."

"Another theory, Silas? Be careful," she lazily teased him; "what we most abuse, you know, is often what we most fear."

"I shall break them," he growled.

"What! your sister-in-law? that frail-looking little thing?"

"She, and. . . her lover."

"Silas, you scare me sometimes, you speak so savagely."

"Scare you, my lady? even you?"

"Why 'even me'?"

"You've explored me," he said grudgingly; "you know me so well."

"Do I? everything about you?"

"Not quite," he said, in a tone of profound gloom.

"Do you know yourself, I wonder?"

"To the depths," he replied.

"Do you enjoy having such complete self-knowledge?"

"It's lonely," he said, his face drawn.

"Lonely, but you have *me* now to talk to."

"Oh, your ladyship is very kind and gracious," he said, with the deferential manner he sometimes abruptly assumed, and through which she always uncomfortably suspected the sarcasm; "I am very grateful to your ladyship. But your ladyship. . ." and thus far he preserved his deference, but abandoned it now to exclaim as though tormented, "You're a whetstone to my disquiet; you taunt me, you keep all peace from me."

"I never knew you wanted peace."

He was tired and dispirited that day, and had been dwelling upon his blindness; he craved for peace, for someone to give him peace!—and she knew it. But she must whip and provoke him back to the strain of his old attitude. She did not know what urged her to say as she did, in her most sneering tone, "I never knew you wanted peace."

"Nor I do," he snarled; "I wouldn't have it as a gift."

III

SO THEY WRANGLED ALWAYS; INDISPENSABLE she might be to him, but peace was certainly not what she brought him. And although they maintained the disguise afforded by her tone of slight condescension, and by his of conventional respect, underneath this disguise fomented the perpetual and manifold contest, of class against class, of the rough against the fastidious, of the man against the woman. She had very little real fear that its full strength would ever break over her,—little real fear, only enough to provide the spice she exacted. She trusted to her appraisement of him: too proud to risk a rebuff; too fiercely recalcitrant under the thongs of affection. Under their menace he snorted and reared, while she laughed indolently, and incited him to further indignations. Yet she held him, she held him! and though she knew full well that she fretted and exasperated him, she held him still; seeing his struggles, but toying with him, pretending to let him go, pulling him back, distracting and confusing his spirit that was always beating round in the search for escape; and all the while she heard from various quarters the pleasant flattery of her guilt extolled under the name of charity.

IV

"You'll be happy soon: you'll have the spring," Silas said to Nan. He did not speak with the customary note of derision in his voice,—this was the newer Silas,—but she thought she detected it very painstakingly concealed.

She went away from him, and her going was after the manner of a flight. Had she followed her impulse, she would have gone running, with her head bent down between her protecting hands. It seemed that she could keep nothing from Silas; he laid his grasp without mercy upon her shyest secrets. She had tried to keep her joy in the coming spring a secret; although reserve was hard of accomplishment to her, she had achieved it, hiding her delight away in her heart, or so she believed, not knowing that her laughter had rung more clearly, or that she had been singing so constantly over her work in the two cottages. She was conscious of no impatience and no desires. She would not, by a wish, have made herself a month older. She was happy now, she told herself, because the country would presently become a refuge from the factory, instead of its dismal and consonant setting, wide and level as the sea itself, in its centre the sinister hump of the abbey and the factory. By walking a little way in the opposite direction, and turning her back upon the village, she would dismiss the factory and look across the liberated country, as it was impossible to do in these days when the floods accompanied the factory for miles around as a reflection of its spirit. She told herself that she wanted nothing more. She knew that she could be happy,—perhaps not indefinitely, but she did not look far ahead, the present was too buoyant and suspended,—happy for the moment if Silas would but leave her alone.

V

FOR A FEW DAYS HE kept up his new smooth-spoken tone; it was "little Nan" this, and "little Nan" that, and whenever he could get hold of her hand he stroked and patted it, and joined his fingers round her wrist, saying that it was fragile. "You're very slight, Nan," he said, feeling her arm and shoulder, and once he laid one hand against her chest and the other against her back, and said that there was no thickness in her body. She withdrew herself, shuddering, from his touch. "I'm blind, you know," he whined, and then laughed, "Bless you, blind or not blind, I know any of you in the room before you've spoken; there's very little Silas doesn't know. I know all about you, Nan, and I'm a good friend to you, too." "But Silas. . ." she began desperately. "Hush!" he said, putting his fingers to her lips and looking mysterious, "no need to say anything; we understand one another." Just then Linnet Morgan came in, throwing aside his cap, and Nan clasped her hands in terror lest Silas should continue. "Linnet?" said Silas instantly, "you're back early today."

Linnet had work which could as easily be done at home. He began at once getting books and papers out of his cupboard, and disposing them on the table. He and Nan observed one another stealthily and quickly; he saw that she wore her dark red shirt and black skirt, and that on his entrance she had become silent as though confused, but meanwhile he talked to Silas and made him laugh, and ran his fingers backwards through his hair. Nan noticed that his crisp hair was quite golden at the roots, and that a fine white line followed the beginning of its growth. He was very fair-skinned, and the back of his neck where it disappeared into his collar was covered with a fine golden down. He was always busy; when he was not working he was talking and laughing; Nan supposed that he had never in his life had time to think about himself.

"There's something I've always wanted to know," began Silas, resting his arms upon the table as though he were watching Nan and Linnet, "what were you two doing here the night Martin came? while I was at the Abbey?"

"The night the donkey was maimed?" asked Morgan.

"Why, fancy you remembering that!" said Silas negligently.

"I was clearing up, and we talked for a bit," Nan put in.

"There was nothing to clear up; it was Sunday evening and you'd been singing and playing your zither. You talked mostly,—now, didn't you?"

"Why not?" asked Morgan. He was very rarely sharp in speech, but he saw Nan's discomfort.

"Why not, indeed? you and Nan are much of an age," Silas replied. They considered him wonderingly; was he well-intentioned or infinitely malign? As they considered him he got up and went towards the stairs. "Back in a moment," he said. They heard his tread upon the steps, then moving overhead. They looked at one another.

"Why did you say that about the donkey?" Nan asked.

"You think, like me, that Silas did it," he answered, as a statement. "Don't look so frightened," he went on, his eyes softening into his ready smile; "I assure you, you need never be frightened of Silas. There's no muscle in his violence. Nothing will ever come of it—beyond maiming donkeys. Oh yes, it's horrible, I know, because it's so futile. No, don't shake your head—your pretty head," he added inaudibly. An impulse came over him to cry "You tiny thing! you slip of fragility!" but he repressed it.

She uttered the most treacherous remark she had ever breathed about Silas, something which fringed the frightful truth, "I know better," then terrified of her indiscretion, added, "Oh no, I mean nothing."

"You are afraid of him, aren't you?" he said, coming round the table closer to her, his attitude very sympathetic and protective, and differing by a shade from Calthorpe's attitude. "You must not be that. One can only be sorry for Silas, who has grown warped and crooked, and who talks because there is nothing else he can do. Whenever I think of Silas, I feel so lucky in mind and body."

She glanced at him gratefully. He had had the tact not to urge an explanation of her injudicious remark, and she knew that she could always depend upon this gentle tact; moreover, he had rescued her soul from the terror she so dreaded, and had by his words set Silas in a sane and pitiful light. It suited her temperament to have Silas drawn down from the uncomfortable heights where he seemed to dwell in perpetual strife with elements. It was no longer Silas who brooded over them, but they who endured and even loved Silas with widened charity. She was very grateful to Linnet for this. What he had done once he could do again; he could soothe her terrors. She had not yet thought of him in so human, companionable a way.

He continued the line that he had taken up, giving her time to command herself fully, making no demands upon her and pretending that nothing had been amiss. He swung himself on to the table, and talked easily,—

"I feel so lucky and thankful for having whole limbs and a sane mind. I don't covet genius, but I do covet sanity; in fact, I'm not sure that the broadest genius isn't the supreme sanity. Balance and justice! I think those two things are magnificent and grand," (but he himself, she knew, would in practice always be merciful rather than just).

"I wish I had your book-learning," she said; "you ought to stick to books."

"Oh no," he replied, "I like chemistry better, and those things. Science. . . If I hadn't to earn my living I shouldn't be working on scents in this factory. No! I'd be in a country cottage with a laboratory."

"You do your best as it is," she said, touching his stack of scientific books.

"I had a bit of training at Edinburgh University," he said, in wistful reminiscence, "but one ought to dedicate years. . ."

"Who was your father?" she asked after much deliberation whether she might venture the question. She knew Morgan only as an isolated person, who had arrived one day into the world of the factory, and had never mentioned home or relations. She knew only that he was Scotch; he had a very slight Scotch accent.

"He was an Inverness crofter," he replied vaguely, "I used to keep the sheep on the hills in mists and snows, and properly I hated it. The days were short, and I thought it was always winter. I used to sit shivering on the brae-side, huddled in a plaid for shelter under a boulder, trying to read while I kept one eye on the sheep. The pages of my book used to get damp and limp, and the print got blurred when I tried to dry the page with the corner of my jacket. Then somebody found out that I wasn't getting any education, and reported it, so I was sent back to school, and was happy again. And you—you haven't lived here always, have you?"

"Since I was ten," she replied, sighing, "we used to live in the south before that. . . I liked that," she said, "it was a pretty place, Midhurst, near Arundel—perhaps you know it?" She thought innocently, and rather in the fashion of a child, that everyone must know what she knew.

"I wish I did, but I don't."

"Oh, it's under the Downs. Do you remember the day we walked with Silas to Thorpe's Howland? that put me in mind of Midhurst; there were woods round about Midhurst."

"You enjoyed yourself that day, didn't you?"

He expected a little burst of rhapsody from her, but she only said quietly, "Yes, I did," and he was aware of disappointment, and at the same time of the little stinging charm of her occasional unexpectedness.

"We both come from sheep country, then," he said, but the images evoked in their minds were different: his of rough hills with their summits lost in mist, and lochs lying amongst the windings at their base; of dirty huddled flocks swept by wind and sleet; while hers were of cropped downland under a blue and white open sky, with the shadows of the clouds bowling across the downs and over the clumps of trees and little church-steeples in the valleys. He realised the disparity, saying "When I say that, we see different pictures," and he smiled, but in his heart he longed for their childhood to have run side by side either in the Sussex or the Highland village. "Have you ever been back there?" he asked.

"Oh no; it's a long way from Lincolnshire. I was always at the factory after I left school, and then when I was eighteen Mother died and I married."

"Only eighteen?"

"A week after my birthday."

"How young!" he said, with such rich and wondering compassion that she looked suddenly as it were into the depths of a cool inexhaustible well, always at hand for the quenching of her thirst. He was sitting on the table near her, while their conversation flowed on in its effortless interest, so that time and his books were forgotten. He seemed quite absorbed in what they were saying, looking down at her with intent consideration. They had attained an intimacy in which they could talk untroubled; she found it very precious.

"Now, Linnet!" said Silas's bantering voice, "making love to my sister-in-law?"

VI

SILAS BECAME UNWONTEDLY WITHDRAWN INTO himself, neither Nan nor Morgan knew what to make of him. At times he avoided them, at other times silently sought their company. Gregory, to whom Nan turned, after one glance at his brother, replied, "Let him alone," and she followed the brief formula as being the best advice, finding that Silas only snarled at her whenever she spoke to him. She was relieved rather than dismayed; Silas surly was preferable to Silas honeyed.

He roamed alone, spending hours in the abbey after dusk; or ordered up Hambley, and under the little man's guidance made his way to the secluded summer-house at Malleson Place. Lady Malleson was also at a loss to understand his altered manner; towards her he relaxed his taciturnity, and his speech was more than ever wild and varied, but although he ranged erratically she had the impression that his mind rarely departed from one central subject, and she had also the shrewd idea that that subject was his little sister-in-law, whom she had once seen, and whom she vaguely thought a pretty, delicate, rather appealing girl, unimportant until she had become the preoccupation of Silas's thoughts.

So long as she had Silas with her, however, she cared very little what he talked about. The utmost that she deplored, sometimes, was his restlessness. It made her wonder whether she really held him. She wondered, indeed, sometimes whether her hold on him was too light to satisfy her vanity, or too secure—all too secure!—for the preservation of her safety and her convenience. She liked danger well enough, but there was a point where danger might become too dangerous.

"Wild man,—Ishmael," she said to him.

But he went on regardless with what he had been saying.

"There's but one use for the body," he exclaimed, "health. Not mortification—that's morbid. But *health*, lean and hard. Sinews like whips." He bared a magnificent forearm. "The only instance where I practise what I preach," he added bitterly, causing the muscles to rise at will.

"Then you should respect your brother Gregory," she said, languidly content.

"You have seen him lately, my lady?"

"Yesterday, in the village."

"The neatest of minds, in the body of a blacksmith," said Silas.

"Neat?"

"Why, yes—so long as he doesn't break out. Then he lays all around him, smashes everything he can see, without comment—that makes it quite uncanny, I assure you—and in a trice returns to his quiet and his neatness as though nothing out of the way had happened. He's very inaccessible, my brother Gregory. No warnings. No explanations. No remorse. Nothing apparently, but action."

"You respect that," she said, looking at his fine bony face, and his thick rough hair.

"Think, if a man's killed," he brooded, "killed by violent means, what an outrage on the body. Blood spilt, that ran secretly and private in his veins. Bones, no one had ever seen. Entrails. What a bursting!"

She pictured his mind as a landscape ravaged by war, here a wreckage of stone and twisted iron, there a grave, here the stark Calvary of a stricken tree, there the bright blare of poppies striving for life amongst the rushes and rank weeds.

"You waste yourself," she said; "you should be a martyr,—or a poet."

She liked to stir him, by such calculated remarks.

"A second-rate poet? not I," he sneered instantly; then, as the flattery stole over him, "More likely a martyr, of the two," he said, responding.

"You waste yourself," she repeated, drawing meanwhile slowly through her fingers the long silk fringe of a shawl that lay thrown across her sofa, "you waste yourself, out of contempt. You eagle with broken wings!"—she knew with what gluttony he accepted such metaphors, and amused herself when he wasn't with her by thinking out new ones that she might serve up to him,—"you repudiate comfort, don't you, in your dream of grandeur. Will you end, I wonder, by getting neither?" "No one speaks to me like your ladyship," he muttered reluctantly. She laughed. She enjoyed pretending to an ideal of him that, his pride well fired, he would strain himself to live up to; an ideal, moreover, that coincided so adroitly with his own ideal of himself. "I never knew a man so vigorously reject the second-best. It was a pity," she continued, smoothing out and patting down the fringe of the shawl, "that you never came across a woman to suit you." She raised her eyes to watch him as she talked, and modulated her phrases according to the expression she found on his face, nor did she trouble to conceal the busy mischief in her own; there were advantages, certainly, in his blindness. "How would you have behaved, I wonder?" she went on; "you would have made a stormy lover, I fancy, once your resistance had been thrown to the winds. Stormy and exacting. Poor woman! Yet I dare say she wouldn't have minded. Women are like that, you know. And for you,— no more loneliness, no more unsatisfied longings, no more misanthropy. I believe you'd have grown into a different man. You would probably have achieved a good deal. . . But it would have taken a clever woman, a very clever woman, to steer you without your knowing that you were being steered."

"Women in my walk of life don't have time for cleverness, my lady," he said acrimoniously, giving a literal answer to her words because he must ignore the meaning which he read into them, and which, as he well knew, she had intended him to read. Her ingenuity was tireless over insinuations that put him on the rack. Clever, she had said; she was clever enough! why hadn't they, he wondered, appointed women to sit upon the tribunals of the Inquisition? "If you had been born into my class, or I into yours. . ." he burst out.

"I don't admit impertinence, you know, Dene," she said in a voice of ice, "and anyway I am afraid I cannot give you anymore time at present."

VII

THUS, ALWAYS. HE HATED HIS bondage, he despised while he coveted the woman, he hated her for holding him bound, but nothing, nothing was comparable to his hatred and disgust of himself in his inability to get free. Often he raved audibly, shaking his fists; and those who saw him stopped to listen to his mutterings, and thought what an alarming sight Silas Dene presented, with his wild blind eyes and furrowed mouth that mumbled and let drop the tiny river of saliva. He was often to be seen thus in the abbey, of an evening, prowling in the aisles; where occasionally on a Sunday he would be perceived by the rare visitor attracted to Abbot's Etchery, that strange island of factory and Norman abbey emerging amidst the floods, sufficiently singular to be worth the journey out from Lincoln; and those who saw him there went away saying that not the least arresting sight in the desolate encampment was the blind man who in savagery and loneliness haunted the precincts of the abbey, and whose incoherent ravings could be readily changed by a little encouragement into a tirade of such vehemence, such angry bitterness, such bewildering aggression. They went away wondering what ailed him, to have made of him so baffling and solitary a figure.

VIII

RUMOUR, AT THE SAME TIME, began to trot like a jackal round the figure of Silas. There was the incident, never very clear to the village, of the fire. Loyalty of course silenced Nan and Morgan; and Hambley, to a very large extent silenced through fear, dared do no more than drop hints that Silas could scarcely trace back to him. Nevertheless, a taste of the story got about, a taste that the village relished and rolled over on its tongue, both in the workshops and the public bar,—for gossip that penetrated the fiercely secluded house of the Denes, and brought to light even the tip of one of their buried secrets, had a legendary smack denied to topics more vulgar and more frequently accessible.

Also, Lady Malleson's name was murmured, behind the shelter of a raised hand.

Nan was aware of the curious looks, thrown at her because she had been with Silas during the fire; and Morgan, aware of similar looks, met them with a contemptuous impatience; but Silas for some days knew of nothing amiss. Only when he stood up to speak at the debating-club, down in the concert-room, he heard a murmur pass through his audience, a murmur of resentment and disapproval. It was as though the accumulated resentment of the men, repressed hitherto out of a lack of understanding, a certain awe, and even a grudging admiration, had now broken its bonds under a definite provocation that had submerged their submission by arousing their disgust. It was a low murmur, compounded of irritation, criticism, and of mutiny under a tyranny they no longer respected and were therefore no longer prepared to admit. Silas heard it, and with his fist already lifted for his peroration, stopped himself dead.

He faced them, standing alone under the dark frown of many sulky and rebellious looks.

"Someone spoke?" he demanded.

He was accustomed to exact silence when he took up the debate.

He had very little time to decide his course of action; he knew that they were against him; knew, obscurely, why; and dared not press home the question.

Morgan was not present, or he might have tided over the matter, out of pity for Silas, who in his defiance looked so extraordinarily gaunt and solitary, and so undefeatably proud.

Morgan, however, was busy elsewhere, so that Silas faced only a lowering throng, that sat obstinate, chins thrust forward into palms and murmured still, with deliberate intent to affront, but without the courage to bring clear accusation.

"This isn't the treatment I'm accustomed to receive here," Silas bayed at them finally, "and until I'm invited I'll no longer trouble you. Invited

I said, and invited I meant. If I'm sought up at my own house perhaps I'll reconsider it, and come back to you. For the present, goodnight to you all."

One, more kind-hearted than the rest, and perhaps ashamed, rose clumsily to intercept him as he went towards the door.

"I'll help you, Dene."

Silas thrust him aside, and strode away alone.

IX

When this story had come to the ears of Nan and Morgan, they whispered "The fire!" and crept away from one another sooner than disturb a subject of which they could not bear to speak.

The fire had taken place at night, and had not been in itself of any importance. "You see nothing but a few tarred sheds burning," Silas had cried, in a frenzy of desperation to Morgan, "and folk will come to me tomorrow to say you acted gallantly, or what not. Why shouldn't you, seeing only wood and flames? You don't hear it coming after you with great light strides and flaming fingers. . ."

"Silas, you're afraid," Morgan had said gravely.

Silas had checked himself at that; he had quavered, and made an effort to recover. The accusation had fallen like a plummet into the uncontrolled waters of his mind. He had quavered, and almost gibbered at Morgan; so greatly fallen beneath his normal standard of pride and independence that he had been shocking to hear and see. He had tried to defend himself, "Not afraid, only helpless, helpless. . ."

Nan and Morgan had stood, hearing him beseech them not to leave him. Nan knew then that Silas was betrayed by fear into revealing something he usually kept very, very carefully concealed; that was why the exposure was so shocking and so degrading; and Morgan seeing it with her eyes stood beside her, both equally hurt, and equally craving to rescue Silas. But he, in his mingled panic and resentment, had had nothing but insults for them, and, nearly screaming, told Morgan to clear out.

"Shall I stay with you?" Nan had asked.

He had hesitated; he wanted to fling her out, he tried to make himself say, "No, go!" but his extreme terror was stronger than this flicker of his other, antagonistic. He said, "Yes, you can stay," a heat of hatred for her passing over him as he said it.

X

THEY HAD SAT IN SILENCE after Morgan had gone, because Silas had forbidden her to speak. She was glad of the hush, for she felt that she had passed through a great empty din and that the brass vacancy of cymbals was still clanging in her ears. The scene had wounded her, and had roused emotions that bewildered her. Why should she resent (to the extent of stretching out deterrent hands, as she had done), the betrayal of Silas by himself? Somewhere, though she would neither have probed nor acknowledged, she had believed that underneath her fear and pity lay hatred of Silas; she had even tried to extend her pity into a reassuring mental scorn. Yet to him, who never spared others, she had had the impulse to cry, "Spare yourself." She had suffered from seeing him untrue to his own tradition.

They sat in silence, Silas tearing at the seat of a rush-bottomed chair, Nan watching the unequal glow in the sky outside the windows. She found herself trembling from time to time. Not with fear of the fire, but with disgust and regret of that noisy scene. She wished that something would happen to restore him to his ancient formidable credit, something to remove that disquieting sense of his fraudulence. She turned away from him, but next moment was glancing at him again; he was destroying the seat of the chair, shred by shred, his fine hands pulling at the rushes with a peevish haste and his head bent obstinately away from observation. Everytime a siren hooted he hunched himself more closely together, as though the compression of his limbs would afford him some protection.

"I think the glare is dying down, Silas," she said gently.

He hunched himself fretfully away.

He was thinking, "They are full of forbearance and long-suffering. Am I to be taught gratitude? perhaps through disaster? They would let God himself look into every corner of their minds. Little children!" For the moment, under the effect of his fear, he did not brand them as lacking in savour. Their limpidity seemed to him as desirable as the absence of danger. If danger might but be removed he would abandon as the price his own arrogant passions. He was humbled now to another standard of life. Weary of battle and opposition, peace appeared to him sweet and seemly, now that he had been granted tumult,—a tumult not of his own making, and entirely out of the control of his stage-managing. He thought again, "They have never a quick word against me. Nan gave me a stick, and I broke it and said I wanted no stick, because I knew she expected me to show pleasure. I am sure that after I broke it she had tears in her eyes. But why should she try to coax me with presents? or I allow myself to be coaxed?" He shuddered at the long scream of a siren, and reflected that they had probably kept the extent of the fire from him, knowing that he could not verify. For an instant he caught hold of the idea that the fire might get across the village to the abbey, and destroy that; and a little flash of old wicked glee passed across him. But it died away. He imagined the fire travelling down his own street, men and women flying before it, and he himself forgotten, engulfed,—perhaps even purposely left to perish. At this point he spoke, "Are you there, Nan?" She was there. "I never meant you any harm, Nan," he said surprisingly. Warm-hearted, she was at his side as the words left his lips. "No, Silas, I know that. . ." "That'll do," he said pushing her away.

But he had now started upon another train of thought, which he adopted and amplified with his usual vehemence. "God preserve me, and I will live to befriend Nan and Linnet." Obscurely he had the instinct of propitiation, offering his intention as a bribe to a very angry god; and partially in his chastened mood,—albeit but the vile chastening of terror,—he yielded to the stirrings of his own repressed sentimentalism. Simplicity, limpidity, were perhaps not the poor and bloodless attributes he had thought. Their case might be turned convincingly by a skilful advocate. He, Silas, had the mettle of strife within him; those other two had not: (The fire! the fire! in the meanderings of his arguments he had almost forgotten the fire. In the rush of recollection he knotted his fingers together till they cracked. He was horribly afraid.) Those two did not fight and wrestle with chimeras, muscles knotted and sweat pouring, as Silas did. Their minds were not ridden by demons. They did not sight everywhere a portent, a dark enemy or a fiercely fair ally. He had scorned them as easy, milky, satisfied,—he knew well the run of the familiar epithets. He had tried to scorn them; he had forsworn their kindness. He had crushed his love for them, and his longing to allow the warm tide of that love to flow in solace over him. He had been proud, and had driven his craft ever to sea, courting the gales and riot, rather than accept the broad comfort of the haven. Proud! proud! how superbly proud! how proportionately base the physical fear that could humble such a spirit of arrogance in man!

XI

A CRY FROM NAN BROUGHT him to his feet, chattering. "What it it? what is it?" in a renewed access of fear. "Oh, Silas!" she exclaimed, coming close to him, "there's Hambley looking in through the window; tell him to go away, oh, please tell him to go away! He does what you tell him always."

Hambley was indeed pressing his face against the window, and the shape of his head was dark against the red sky. He was so small that he was only just able to reach the window by climbing to the outside sill with the tips of his fingers, and the end of his nose was flattened white upon the pane. Nan could see the grin on his evil little face. Silas strode to the door, flung it open, and summoned the little man. At the end of the street the night was torn by flames.

As soon as Hambley was inside he seized the little man by his collar. "Now what were you doing, peeping into my house when you thought you wouldn't be found out? You little skunk, I've always called you, and so you are. You frightened Nan, you little skunk. You meant to spy upon me. Well, you'll see what you get!" Holding him easily with one hand, sometimes swinging him clean off his feet, so that he twirled and dangled in mid-air, Silas thrashed him with his fist, and Hambley shrieked and appealed to Nan, and tried, but quite vainly, to kick Silas. Nan got into a corner, out of the way of the blows. When he had finished, Silas carried him over to the door and threw him regardlessly out into the street.

XII

MORGAN CAME BACK AT MIDNIGHT, and said that the fire was over, not having spread beyond the sheds. He was rubbing his blackened hands on a piece of waste. His eyes fell upon the litter of shredded rushes scattered in witness on the floor near Silas. Nan drooped, pale and tired. He began to tell her about the fire, trying to brighten her and to make her feel that she was no longer a prisoner alone with Silas. He was purposely taking no notice of Silas, but presently looked up to see the blind man standing above them.

He appeared to be immensely tall and haggard, and upon his face was a look of suffering, which by the accentuation of furrow and wrinkle gave the suggestion that he was unkempt. His limbs and torso were hugely, grotesquely reproduced in shadow upon the walls and ceiling behind him. Inscrutable to them, he loomed over Nan and Linnet. At last he spoke.

"You're glad to have him back, Nan. You're glad to come back to her, Linnet."

Their eyes met in tremulous surprise; was Silas to serve as their interpreter?

"You little, dainty people! Oh, yes. I know. Gentle in your dealings. Amiable. Indulgent. You don't criticise—criticism's uncharitable— might hurt somebody's feelings. Let things remain as they are; don't disturb. Moderation! That's your creed. Make terms. Compromise!" He dropped exclamations, and swung into his most rhetorical vein, in which he seemed really possessed by a spirit that released the unfaltering words. "O pliant ones of the earth! blessed are the meek, and flowers shall revive at your passage. Wander into the woods; call to the roe-deer to eat from your hand. Look with envy at the pairing foxes, the nesting birds; no creature so wild that it may escape the yearly call of home. If the fox and the vixen together can burrow their earth for shelter and the whelping of their litter, cannot you two together build a hut of boughs and branches in a clearing beside the stream? Listen: I covet no love, I am debarred; and love when it touches men like me is no virtue, only an indulgence of self and a lapse from strength." He laughed. "Who would be weak? or bestial? But in you, love shall attain its highest purpose of usefulness and steadfastness. To be steadfast in love is reserved to man; it is the conscious will of love, the sustained reason. Without it, as well be a dog, and couple in the street. Are you fit? You are young and your minds are counterparts; you have no business with me or with Gregory. Leave me to Gregory, and Gregory to me; the dumb shall lead the blind, and the blind shall speak for the dumb. But you, go out, where no strife assails, and concern yourselves with labour. You are the builders, and we are the destroyers; we are the cursed, and you are the blessed. You and your like must build your security upon the ruins of us and our like; it's the natural law. I might have been another man, but God saw fit to twist me; he wrenched my spirit and upon each of my eyes in turn he laid a finger."

They sat absolutely speechless, confused and confounded that he should thus trumpet out the secret they had hitherto guarded from one another. They had wondered and suffered and trembled much, but of all outcomes this was an outcome they had certainly never foreseen. It broke over them like a natural catastrophe; Silas was making it into something beyond the diapason of their souls.

"Build!" he said passionately, earnestly, "build with your sanity and your health. Leave query and destruction to the tormented spirits; there will always be enough of those; and if you did but know,—oh, world!" he said, clasping his hands, "if you did but know, you would pity the precursor, solitary and bold. Then comes the army of the workers, with honest tools, and their flowing quietness.—Why should you struggle, you two, beside Gregory and me? You should be side by side, perfectly matched, amongst children who should resemble you. Tell me," he said, bending down to them, "you love?"

When he reduced it to those naked terms, they were ashamed into honesty, both towards him and towards each other; they assented, as though he were a priest reading over them a terrible and simple marriage-service.

"Then you shall have the courage to love. You shall go unmolested. You were intended to fulfil, not to renounce. Who pretends to one law for all? Not I; I wouldn't dare utter such a heresy of intolerance. Not in my sane moments. Who would take a field-bird up into the mountains? His place is simpler; sweeter. . ."

He suddenly put his hands over his face, and his voice faltered, as though he were spent and had nothing more to say.

"Go away now," he said fretfully, "I'm tired out."

XI

I

THIS WOUND, THIS GASH, TO be exposed to the village! How greedily they would lick up his blood! they would set upon him with claw and fang as upon a lion brought low. No delight could equal the delight over the dictator shamed, or the eagerness with which those in subjection would pounce upon the infallible taken in fault. But, while knowing the story of the fire to be common gossip, he would grant no concessions; he stalked about the streets in challenging pride, more than usually unkempt, more than usually fierce, an object of whispered comment for all those who had expected him to keep himself at last within bounds. It was noticed that when spoken to, he threw back his head as though it had been crowned with a mane, and his answers were too haughty to be set down as the cheaper insolence. The men were a little impressed, but to give themselves determination they continued to mutter against him. Calthorpe knew it, and was concerned. He hinted something to Sir Robert Malleson, but Malleson had received an anonymous letter which disturbed and occupied every energy of his mind, and was unsympathetic. The only person with whom Calthorpe could get a hearing was Mr. Medhurst, who called at Silas's cottage, and came away saying blandly that Dene was an altered being. Why had Calthorpe so distressed himself over Dene's state of mind, and the attitude of the village? He could not understand. Calthorpe in his kind-heartedness had surely been mistaken.

"Why, Dene, I am very happy to find you in so Christian a spirit." Poor Mr. Medhurst suffered greatly from the trap of his phraseology; it made all intercourse with his fellows a source of self-consciousness so acute that he felt justified in counting every visit as a mortification. Yet he was unable to control it. Visits to Silas Dene were a special mortification; he had to pray for strength before setting out, and now Mrs. Gregory Dene, a good little soul, was not there to help him. "Of course, you are a church-goer; I often see you in the abbey," Mr. Medhurst pursued.

"Yes, sir," Silas replied gravely.

"You seem to prefer the evening services? Ah well, I dare say they fit in better with your work." Silas made no reply, but sat smiling to himself. Mr. Medhurst started another topic, "What pretty flowers you have always in here, Dene."

"Yes, sir, my sister-in-law does that."

"She must be a great comfort to you, Dene, since. . . well, since you have been by yourself. . . you know. . ."

"Since my wife was killed, sir."

"Well. . . yes; yes, after all, that is what I meant. I should like to say, Dene, that I admire extremely the courage you have displayed under your sorrow; I think I may claim that I am not unobservant—although, God knows, sorely wanting in other qualities, I add in all humility. I will confess that your conduct at the inquest impressed me most painfully, but we need not dwell upon that; since then I have had nothing but praise for your demeanour."

"Indeed, sir?"

"Yes, indeed. I was saying so to Sir Robert Malleson only the other day. It gives me great pleasure to say so to you now. You are a brave man, Dene." He pronounced the words "brave man" separately and with emphasis, and allowed a suitable emotion to rise through his tone.

"Thank you, sir."

"Not at all, Dene, not at all. It is only your due."

"Well, sir, perhaps we all have liftings towards honour," said Silas demurely.

"H'm!" said Mr. Medhurst. What strange phrases the man employed! "Liftings towards honour." What could that mean? But he was certainly quieter; quieter and better-mannered, and his frequent presence at evening service was a hopeful sign, though Mr. Medhurst had noticed with a vague misgiving that he took no part in the responses.

II

TWO DAYS AFTER THE FIRE Silas received a summons from Lady Malleson, a summons that he had been expecting because he knew Malleson was away. It was brought to him not by Hambley as usual (that was scarcely surprising), but by Emma, Lady Malleson's maid. Would he come immediately? she, Emma, was to bring him back. "I'll wait for you, Mr. Dene; you'll be wanting to brush up a bit," she said, looking at his dirty hands and untidy hair, but he scoffed at the suggestion and said that they should start at once.

In his impatience he forced the maid to a great pace, dragging her along rather than allowing her to lead him. She kept exclaiming that he would stumble over roots and rabbit-holes as they crossed the park, but he brushed her caution aside. "You're very particular not to keep her ladyship waiting," said she meaningly, not appreciating this walk with blind Dene, of whom so many strange tales were told. Little Hambley had been seen that morning up at Malleson Place, scowling and limping in the stable-yard, and the grooms with much relish had said that Silas Dene had given him a thorough thrashing. Little Hambley had, of course, not owned to it. He had snapped viciously in reply to their chaff. Emma longed to ask Silas whether the story was true, but as no one ever asked questions of Silas, she, like many others, held her tongue.

III

HE WAS TAKEN UP TO the sitting-room, introduced by the maid, and left just inside the door, as on the occasion of his first visit. But now he knew the way about the room.

"In the house today, my lady?" he said, "I like the garden-house better."

"And you want your own way, as usual?" she asked.

"You say that as though you hated me," he said, stopping dead.

"What a sensitive ear you have," she replied cruelly. "I do."

There was a finality about this pronouncement which caused him to take it with the utmost seriousness. Her tones were chill and bloodless and dead, and they disquieted him, so much that he advanced not another step, but remained readjusting his mood, which had been eager, to one of defence. He was horribly startled. It was fortunate for him that he could not see her; she had retreated from him as far as the size of the room would allow, behind the sofa, where she stood shivering as though with cold, her eyes fixed and unblinking, her hand laid upon her loose garment to hold it close at the throat, and all her muscles gathered ready for swift escape at any sign of advance on his part.

"I should not have sent for you," she said, "but I knew you could not read a letter if I wrote you one, and I did not care to send you a message through any of my servants. I don't want to keep you long, as I only want to tell you that I am leaving for London tomorrow and shall not be seeing you again. I could certainly have sent you a message to tell you that. But I wanted to tell you my reason myself."

She had prepared beforehand what she intended to say, for her safeguard lay in frigidity of speech, and to achieve that she must maintain frigidity of feeling. That had been easy before he came; but when she saw him her cold anger had been shaken, her contempt had wavered beneath a return of her old respect, and her audacity in risking danger had revived. "I wanted to tell you my reason," she resumed, "but before doing so I must own that you had completely taken me in. I thought I knew you well, but I knew only that part of you which you were willing that I should know. I thought I had made in you the discovery of something really rather remarkable. I was rather pleased with myself over it. I know now that I have been stupidly mistaken. Your elaborate fraud deceived me as being a genuine thing. . ."

"I can see you have learnt all this by heart," he interrupted. She flamed up no less at his perspicacity than at his rudeness.

"Very well," she cried, "I'll drop my stilted phrases. I did prepare them, but they are true, for all that. I have found you out. You interested me, you even impressed me,—I hate you for it. You're nothing but a sham and a coward."

"It's not true," said Silas, growing very pale.

"It's so true," she said quickly, "that the words I've just used to you are the very words you have always most dreaded hearing. A sham and a coward. You're such a coward that there have been moments when you were glad you were blind, because that saved you from dangers other men were expected to undertake. You were quite safe to talk about danger; your blindness sheltered you, and words couldn't possibly hurt. Am I not speaking the truth? Your blindness has been your best friend, as well as your worst enemy,—your worst enemy, because it favoured your horrible imagination, and provided a darkness that you peopled with shapes; your best friend, because all the time it preserved you from having to practise what you preached. See how I know you now. I suppose it amused you to deceive me, to see just how far you could go, and sometimes when you thought you'd put your foot an inch over the line of my credulity you drew it back very skilfully. Now I have simply found you out for what you are. I have learnt the story of the fire two nights ago."

"Nan!" exclaimed Silas, in a burst of fury.

"Not at all; I have seen Hambley. I don't wish to make any mystery. He came to see me this morning, whining and snivelling, and told me the whole story: how you had lost your head, how you had gibbered with fright—gibbered was the word he used—he says you went like this," and she imitated a man in the extremity of terror, working her mouth, distending her eyes and nostrils, and clacking her fingers; "he was not pretty to watch, Dene. Then he told me how you had dragged him in and beaten him for looking in through your window; he was quite shrewd enough to see that you seized upon the pretext of beating him merely as a relief to your nerves, that fright had exasperated. He came to me in order to be revenged on you, and also, I think, because he wanted to whimper to someone. He says you went upon your knees to young Morgan, and that Morgan was laughing at you, though you didn't know it, and that even your sister-in-law smiled more than once behind her hand. Well, that's the picture I carry away of you, Dene. You can hardly be surprised that I regret the kindness I have shown to you. I have made a great mistake which I shall know better than to repeat in the future." She hardened herself, she mentally insisted on her relief at escaping from a situation which she had felt to be getting beyond her control. There were many incidents she remembered with discomfort, and her husband had been very peremptory, when, the anonymous letter in his hand, he had come to her, "If I thought there was any truth in these revolting hints. . ." yes, decidedly, Hambley's revelations had been very opportune as an excuse for getting rid of Silas. She thought, on the whole, she had manœuvred her opportunities ably.

"Hambley shall pay for this."

"Hambley must take care of himself," she replied, "I have no doubt that you will invent some form of revenge which will interest you very much as a new experiment, and you will improve it and refine it and fiddle over it, like some magician preparing a brew. I should never, at any moment, have had any doubts as to that. I should like you to understand that I always knew you for cruel, unscrupulous, and without heart or conscience; I thought you a ruthless man, but where I went wrong was in not thinking you despicable. I could have respected you for thorough-going villainy,—yes, I thought there was a certain largeness of gesture about your discontent,—but I have only contempt for the sham."

Her voice had grown still more cold and level; it licked sharply round his vanity, and as ever, his instinct flew to physical violence. He snarled, and moved in her direction, knocking over a small table, but she dodged him.

"Keep quiet, Dene," she said, in the same glacial tone, "we really cannot play this ridiculous game of blindman's buff."

IV

He saw that he could do nothing against her, and indeed was too proud to try. His pride had risen correspondingly to his humiliation; he would show her that something, at all events, in him was not a sham. He was terribly, doubly hurt,—hurt in his heart, and hurt, too, with the uneasy wound of pride, his pride towards her, his pride towards himself. All that she had said had been so true; she had found the truth as a weapon, and had beaten him with it across the face. He was so battered, so gashed with scorn, that he was surprised to find himself still alive and sentient. But he *was* sentient. He *was* indomitable. His life was so strong that it had not been knocked even temporarily unconscious. It stirred: he spoke.

"I shall say nothing to justify myself," he began. "If your ladyship wishes to think ill of me you must do so, although I dare say I could alter your opinion." He was prompted to say this by a phrase that had occurred to his mind, and which gave him some private consolation, "I have, after all, murdered my wife, defied God, and banished my own son." But he did not say these words aloud. "You are of course free, my lady," he went on, "to dismiss me without being besought by me. You call me a coward; you forget I have the courage to live alone."

"The egoism," she amended.

"No!" he said sharply, "it's discipline, not inclination, and it began when I was a boy, because I wouldn't have pity. Now it's a habit. I've shut myself off from pity. I'm well schooled."

"Is that all you have to say?" asked Lady Malleson, as he ceased.

"Did you expect me to plead for mercy? You were quite right when you said you knew only the part of me that I was willing for you to know. If you had known everything, my lady, you might have been startled." He was nursing his secret phrase. "But I plan very carefully what I shall betray to different people. Being blind, I must invent things to think about."

"You are a demon!" broke from Lady Malleson.

Silas smiled a bitter, gratified smile; he had at least succeeded in making her angry. Having done so, could he reconquer her? Should he risk the affront of failure? She was all he had. No! if she cared so little, let her go. He would not submit to being patronised, to being kept on sufferance by the woman who alone had the privilege of twisting the strings of his heart. If that privilege, so grudgingly, so agonisingly accorded, were to be so little esteemed, let her go! What matter? A loneliness the more.

"I thought at first that I would tell Emma to bring you to the abbey," she resumed, more quietly; "I thought that the setting would please you and satisfy your sense of histrionics. It would have been so thoroughly Silasian. For you *are* histrionic, aren't you, Silas?"

"Perhaps," he said.

"You and I, sitting on two cane chairs, in the dark abbey," she went on, "while I poured out to you in an undertone all my opinion of you, my new opinion, for the first time, my true opinion, and then, who knows? the organist might have come in to practise, and so provided an accompaniment for your answer. I really believe your answer would have varied according to the music. It would tickle you to sway your life on a dainty chance like that. I wonder that I overcame the temptation."

"A great pity," said Silas indifferently, but as though he had allowed himself to be beguiled a moment by the charm of the suggestion. She was annoyed with herself; she felt that she had allowed her irony to run away with her, to become a little too wild, especially when he continued in a tone of irreproachable conventionality, "I must now thank your ladyship for the kindness shown in the past and for the many hours I have been allowed to spend at Malleson Place. I appreciate that it isn't many poor chaps like me that's given the advantage. It's been a gift blown me by the ill wind of my wife's death and my blindness. Your ladyship has a kind heart,—they all say so in the village when they hear of the favours shown to blind Dene." As he spoke he made small staccato movements with his fingers, bearing a resemblance to the dart of Gregory's pencil in some minute alteration of his designs, a family resemblance, that in its finicky precision was equally incongruous to both brothers; in Silas the gestures seem to indicate the finishing touches to a work of art about to be laid aside; the touches were given, possibly, with regret, but still with a certain affectionate satisfaction, as to work well done, and opportunely completed; (he marvelled at himself even as he spoke and gesticulated); they irritated Lady Malleson with a small, wiry irritation, like some insignificant but exasperating physical pain, causing her to forget what she had called the grandeur of Silas, and to remember only the warped, malicious artistry in which he appeared to take delight.

Then he changed; he towered; he dwarfed her; all her superiority went in a flash.

"Listen," he said then, so suddenly that she had the impression that he had stepped bodily out of a disguise,—"Your interest in me may have been unreal to you,—how could it have been otherwise? You are a fine lady, you have been through many experiences; I'm a rough fellow, and I dare say bitter and brutal enough. . ."

"You like to think yourself brutal, don't you?" she interjected.

"Such as I was," he said, "you had me; are you proud of what you made of me?—Oh!" he said, hearing her movement of impatience, "I won't make you discourse; only that question I wanted to ask you: are you proud of what you made? Only this: was I *so* unworthy of your ladyship? Have you been sullied by my contact? Or have I, by God," he thundered at her, "been sullied by yours? I'm not so sure. What are you wondering in your mind now? whether you can trust me to go away and hold my tongue? You think you won't risk putting the idea of indiscretion into my head; you probably think it will come there quite soon enough by itself. Are you any less of a coward than I? You need have no anxiety, I'm not tempted to revenge myself on you in that way,—you think of that, you're preoccupied with that, but do you think at all of what you may have done to me? You picked me up casually, and you think you can put me down in the same way. But, between picking me up and putting me down, you've worked on me; you don't leave me quite the same as you found me; and I'm not an easy metal."

She was frightened when he said that, and muttered hurriedly, "I hope I haven't done you any harm."

"One doesn't know what harm or good one does," he replied, "working-man or grand lady. You'll go your way. I'm asking you only whether you'll remember me with pride, or whether you'll think of yourself as one of the things that dragged me back, when I was always trying to escape? I'm not strong, you know. I'm not strong. I'm only cursed with a spirit that's totally beyond my strength."

"I don't understand," she said uneasily; she tried to tell herself that he was making a great fuss; but she could not get away from the idea that the "fuss" was tragically weighted.

"You're quite safe," he said, with extraordinary gentleness. "I never wanted to love, you know, either you or anyone else; I often told you so; but it isn't love that I abuse, only the weakness that submits to it. And I have to acknowledge that you are wise in getting rid of me. I'm all awry, you know; misbegotten; and folk like me are better left alone; their misfortune only rubs off on to other people. You are wise to protect yourself; that's always a wise thing to do. I could wish only that you had done it earlier; you would have made it easier for me."

The melancholy of his reproach surprised her into saying, "Is it at this moment that you're speaking from your heart, or was it just now?" and she remembered the sharp finicky gestures he had made when he thanked her for the kindness she had shown him. "To what extent are you theatrical?" she asked, in a little outburst of bad temper.

"That isn't a question I should answer, even if I had the answer at the tip of my tongue," he replied. "You may think, if you choose, that I am never sincere." (She thought, "He is going back to his old manner." She was greatly thankful.) "Perhaps I am no more sincere," he continued, standing there, "than any of your ladyship's little gimcracks in this room." His reference to her gimcracks was not contemptuous; he seemed rather to be translated into a region where a large gentleness held sway. Ironically enough, she thought that she had never seen him before, although this was the last time she was seeing him. A similar idea appeared to strike him at the same moment, for he said, "All along, I have fought against you, and tried to disguise myself from you. It doesn't matter now. I seem always to be fighting,—floundering about,—don't I? I wonder whether I shall ever get away? away from myself? Would your ladyship ring for Emma now? I should like to go."

She got up wearily and crossed the room to the bell. He was standing there, no longer scathing, but quiet, patient, and tired. She looked at him; and, going swiftly to him, she caught his hand.

"Listen, Silas. Perhaps I've been too hasty. Listen to me. Perhaps I need not dismiss you altogether. . . I might reconsider. . ."

"No," he brought out with extreme firmness, as though he extorted from a long way off the last tragic effort of an overstrained will.

"As you please," she said, dropping his hand, and in her angry haste she threw open the door to urge the maid who was coming to lead him away.

XII

I

GREGORY STILL WORKED OBSTINATELY AMONG the vats. Calthorpe had tried to coax him away to the engine-rooms, but got no more answer than a shake of the head. In his secret mind, Gregory was preparing a scheme, now nearly complete, that would reorganise the whole working of the factory; he saw himself as its originator and supervisor, and was far too proud to accept a preliminary post as a unit among a number of mechanics. He was living for the day when, before an assembled board-meeting, he would lay his designs upon the table; although he could not explain them by speech, their beautiful precise simplicity would explain itself while he stood aside, arms folded, and read the effect upon the faces of the directors. (He had tested some designs upon Calthorpe,—not those designs, of course,—and the overseer had been seriously impressed. Gregory knew with calm certainty, untouched by diffidence, that his work was good.) Perhaps he would take Nan with him as interpreter to the board-meeting; she was intelligent, her small fingers flew fast, and it would be a compensation, in some guise, for the hours he had spent away from her in abstraction over his drawings.

Meanwhile, time progressing towards that day, he worked in the gallery of vats. It was a sort of grotesque vigil. He hated the nauseous, automatic work, but obliged himself to keep to it with a strength of mind that Silas wholly appreciated. Day after day he climbed the long iron ladder to the upper gallery, dressed in splashed and grimy overalls, and renewed his occupation, trundling hand-barrows, emptying an over-full or cooling an overheated vat. When he had to do this he stripped to the waist, and stirred and flacked the boiling slime with a weapon shaped like a flail. Sweat ran from him, and in the gaunt gallery of iron girders, amongst the vats of moving yellow fat, the play of his shining muscles and sculptural body stood out as a classical and noble revelation.

Regarding Nan as his chattel, he never wondered whether he was or was not agreeable to her, and in his egoism never noticed her sensitive wilting under his caresses. His pride and his machines were personalities infinitely more living to him than the instrument of comfort and pleasure that was his wife. When he had married her, he had loved her in a rough animal way, that never had in it a streak of consideration or unselfishness; it had amused him to possess as a toy something so weak, so little, and so pretty, and in the first weeks of their marriage he had devised games for his own satisfaction, to pick her up between both hands and lift her till her head touched the ceiling, or to catch her up and run with her along the dyke—such eccentric sports, that half frightened her, half pleased her instinct by his display of strength. Then he had grown accustomed to her flitting presence. He had ceased to raise his head when she came into the room, or to finger with wonderment her small hands, or to turn over with derisive affection the ribbons, cottons, and odds and ends in her work-box. She ceased to be so distinctly, so newly, Nan, and became merely one of the little knot of four living in the double-cottage,—himself, Silas, Nan, and Hannah. He watched her when he had nothing better to do, just as he watched Silas or Hannah, or, nowadays, Linnet, but within the vaults of silence his true life was turned inwards upon himself.

And Silas was studying him; Silas studying Gregory! Communication between them was almost non-existent; Silas could, indeed, write on a piece of paper and Gregory could read the message, but, beyond a clumsy finger-system relating only to elementary practical matters,—names of objects, and such,—Gregory was quite unable to converse with Silas. Silas foresaw therefore that he would have no means of judging the effects of his observations on Gregory's mind. But difficulties only whetted his ingenuity. He needed an occupation and an opiate as he had never needed them before,—not that he allowed himself to own to this,—and the double disaster he had undergone, far from humbling him, stung him to a determination of mischief that welcomed any obstacle as an additional employment for his days. He stood at his work in the shops, before a trestle table, making the square boxes into parcels, and as he tied the string he fancied that every knot secured a further mesh in the net he was weaving round unsuspecting lives.

II

BUT ALL THE WHILE HE was gnawed by sorrow for what he was doing. Nan! Linnet! so young, so disarming! he knew he loved them both. In his mind they were children. Could he but struggle out of the deadly groove of perversity that held him, could he but shake off the innumerable fetters of his small malignities! As well hope to shake off the physical cowardice that was his secret torment and his shame. To rise! to escape! to leave behind all the indignity of petulance and rancour! at times he fancied almost that he could hear the beating of great wings, and a kind of swoon overtook him, as one who has fasted, or has remained too long in mystic contemplation; but, emerging from it, he was instantly wrapped up again in the cold craftiness of his schemings, that tangled themselves round him as surely as he would tangle them round others.

III

HE MUST FORGET LADY MALLESON. He wished that the cause of his disgrace could have been different; those words, "a coward and a sham," left a bad taste in his mouth; there was no getting round them, and no getting round the incident of the fire; he wished passionately that the whole thing might be blotted out: there was Nan's knowledge, Morgan's knowledge, Lady Malleson's knowledge,—that was the worst,—and lastly Hambley's knowledge, but his contempt for Hambley was so great that he could disregard everything from that quarter. But he could not pretend to himself to disregard the knowledge of those other three; it infuriated and mortified him. Lady Malleson knew him for what he was; knew him for worse than he was, despised him more than he deserved. He had to bear this, added to his loss of her; and he found it hard. Once his angry pain drove him to write to her, as lackadaisical a letter as he could compose, flicking at her the phrases that he had been slightly drunk on the occasion of his last interview with her; that he apologised for presenting himself to her in that condition, also for whatever wild statement he might have uttered; he sent the letter; in his mind he followed its journey; he wept bitter and angry tears on the morning when it must be received.

IV

WARILY, ABOVE ALL, MUST HE tickle Gregory's suspicions.

No one knew of the system that grew up then in that house. The house was secret enough at anytime; now it contained a secret within its secret. It contained the pursuit of Gregory by Silas, the difficult tracking-down, the requisite, progressive measure of suggestion, the pieces of paper bearing the poison of a phrase, the impotence of the dumb man, his efforts to escape from his tormentor, then his return in his cravings for a greater certainty. Silas was intent upon his own skill; a touch here, a touch there; he placed them with a sharp and delicate artistry. His only fear now was that Gregory might refuse to go with Calthorpe, and to forestall that danger he got hold of the overseer.

"I hope, Mr. Calthorpe, you'll keep Gregory to this job. You know he's diffident,—to look at the way he sticks to those vats, he who's fit to manage the engine room!—and now he's saying that you're wanting him to go out of charity, like, and if he thinks that, he won't be beholden to you."

"I'll go in to him now, and fix it up once for all. There's no charity about the matter; I don't want Gregory to *talk* to the plants, I want him to *look* at them."

"I knew I only had to mention it to you," said Silas demurely.

<h2 style="text-align:center">V</h2>

GREGORY WAS TORN. HE WAS bitterly unwilling to forego the chance offered to his solitary ambition. He was forty-five, and he had given the whole of his youth to the patient, meticulous study of machinery; could he decline the chance, on the strength of a few words from Silas,— roguish, busy old Silas! always meddling at something, never letting well alone—a few words that perhaps were rooted in nothing but Silas's imagination? No, he couldn't decline it! But what if Silas were right? Nan was young, Morgan was young, he constantly saw them talking together, talking when Nan should have been working and when Morgan, more naturally, might have been kicking a ball with other young men on the green. Here he became full of gloom. Should he charge Nan with it? no, women were too artful; he would learn nothing through charging Nan. Better to trust Silas, then by the time he came back from Birmingham Silas could tell him as a sure fact whether or no. . . For the first time he began to think of the consequences, of the obligation that might be laid upon him. . . Perfectly honest, he envisaged facts unflinchingly, in the sole light under which they offered themselves to him. He was not a man to admit alternatives.

He had only one slight hesitation: was it fair to lay a trap for Nan? But he discarded the doubt. If she were innocent no trap could catch her; if she were guilty, he had the right to protect his interests as best he might; he and Silas both had that right. They were both handicapped; their whole lives were, in some measure, the lives of animals at bay.

VI

H E   S P E N T   T H E   I N T E R V A L   B E F O R E   his departure in making observations for himself, prowling round when he might least be expected, entering his house, suddenly and noiselessly, or even looking in through the window,—which, being tall, he could do with ease,—and sometimes on these occasions he saw Nan and Morgan together, talking, in the midst of their occupations, but he never saw more than that. To see them talking was, however, a source of exasperation to him; he fancied that the most tender words were passing between them under his very eyes, an affront, an outrage, that drove him to gnaw his finger-tips in the same way that Silas did, and to fly the house lest his black looks should arouse their vigilance. His behaviour became wild and unaccountable. When he was alone with Nan, he turned roughly demonstrative, while behind his caresses lay the intention of finding out whether she would wince. It was all too clear to him that she did wince. More than once he was upon the point of questioning her, and again upon the point of refusing to leave with Calthorpe, but he crushed these impulses. If he remained, he might never know, so wily and circumspect would they be; if he went, they would throw off much of their caution before blind Silas. Silas was a good watch-dog, who in ten days would nose out certainty. To the suspense of those ten days Gregory would expose himself; a martyrdom which he undertook in the bleak spirit of a martyr, grimly, without heroics, in the stern desire to win truth at the cost of pain.

She winced—oh yes! she winced. She turned away from him, said he bothered her, kept herself unnecessarily busy. The more she evaded him, the less willing was he to leave her alone; he followed her when she fled into the scullery, and with a gasp she became aware of his silent presence as his hands were laid from behind upon her shoulders. This was a persecution worse than the verbal persecution she had endured from Silas! She prayed ardently and with terror for the day when he should go. The ten days' reprieve stretched luminous as a lifetime—but even then there would be Silas, Silas honeyed again, when, all her wits cried to her, he was fifty times more dangerous. She thought that without Linnet she would have become truly distracted; yet even to Linnet, at home, she dared not speak overmuch. She could have kissed the forewoman of her department who again sent her to his room with a message.

V. SACKVILLE-WEST

VII

SHE KNOCKED AT HIS DOOR with no less timidity than she had done the first time, her hand clasping her beating heart. His voice called "Come in!"; she slipped in; his dim room and the shining alembics were lovely and mysterious, like a fairy-story, after the chill of the bare linoleum-lined passage she had just followed. In a moment they were close to one another, their fingers wove together without knowing how it had so come about; the fact of being unexpectedly alone came like a draught of water to the thirsty.

"I hate that passage leading to your room—it's like a prison," she murmured, raising her hand to his bright hair; "it so cool and dim in here; I wish, oh, how I wish I could work in here helping you."

"It might be arranged. . ." he began enviously.

"Oh no," she said, shaking her head, "we mustn't think of it."

"We're never really alone," he said.

"No."

They looked at each other gravely and pitifully.

"It does seem so hard," her small voice took up again, "that you and I, who have never done any harm, should be spied on and hunted, because that's what I feel: hunted. We haven't done any harm, have we? only in our thoughts, that is," she amended, scrupulous, "and even then I don't think it's terrible harm to wish we might sometimes be alone. I try not to wish for more than that, Linnet; I do indeed. You mustn't come so close to me, please," and she put out her hand to push him away a little.

"Why mustn't I?"

"You know quite well: I can't bear your nearness."

"Nan, you are the most provoking mixture of frankness and prudery. . ."

"I don't mean to be. I came straight to you when I got into the room, because I was happy and forgetful, but I am sorry; that wasn't encouraging you to behave as I want you to behave. You know what I tell you: we can *talk*, no more."

"But talk can lay up trouble too, you know, Nan."

Her face took on a startled look, as a dismayed child's.

"What! do you mean we ought to give that up too? Oh, no, Linnet, I couldn't bear that, indeed I couldn't; you mustn't suggest it."

"Of course I don't suggest it; is it likely? Only I think you trick yourself into believing what you want to believe, and if your conscience does prick you, you try to salve it—and I dare say succeed—by imposing some quite hypocritical limitation."

"Are you laughing at me or not? Or are you serious? do you mean that I ought not to see you at all or talk to you? perhaps you are right. . ."

"Nan, you are too perverse! I only mean that if you allow yourself to talk to me, and allow me to talk to you, and to make love to you, you might consistently allow me to go further, to take your hand, for instance, without pushing me away when I stand quite respectfully beside you."

"I see what you mean; I can't argue, but I think, please, I would rather go on in the same way as before."

"Very well," he said ruefully.

"And why do you say 'make love'?" she harked back after a little. "As though it were just a way of spending the time? Anyway, I think I would rather you did not; we can talk quite well without that, and then you need not think I am hypocritical."

"You do keep me in order, Nan, don't you?" he said.

"No, I am often very weak and cowardly."

"You are only cowardly when you won't face what is to become of us," he replied, with more seriousness.

Again she looked startled.

"Oh, please, Linnet, I don't like talking about that."

"Well, but, my dear," he said, "you know quite well that we cannot go on indefinitely as we are at present; you ought to be the first to realise it, with your scrupulous mind always splitting hairs and dwelling on niceties. If it were light come, light go, between us—there a kiss and here an arm round you—it would be different. But you know it is not like that. It is perhaps your very prudery that puts the whole thing on a different footing. Anyway you know that it is a matter of all our lives. . ."

"Yes, it is, isn't it?" she said, with a contented sigh, and leaning up against him.

"Nan, you distract me!" he exclaimed, "I say that it is for all our lives, and you murmur with pleasure, as though the whole thing were thereby settled. In the meantime I am neither one thing nor the other; I am neither your friend, nor your husband, nor your lover."

"Oh, but you are surely. . ."

"Well, what am I? I wish I knew!"

"My lover," she said in a low voice.

"Nan, don't hang your head so; for pity's sake don't; you are too charming when you do it. No, I am not your lover. . . worse luck. . ."

　　　　　　　　V. SACKVILLE-WEST

"But you do love me, don't you?"

"Good God, do you doubt it?"

"Well, you never say so. You never said it. Silas had to say it for you."

"But I've said so since."

"Oh. . . *since!*" she said.

"But, my darling Nan, a little way back you forbade me to speak of love to you."

"Yes, you see," she said with another sigh, less contented, this one, "I want to have nothing on my conscience, nothing, nothing, nothing— except my thoughts, and I can't help those."

"Won't you tell them to me?"

"If I told them to you, they would be on my conscience, and that's where I don't want them to be."

"You are deplorably logical, when it is for my undoing," he said, sighing in his turn.

"If I had a laden conscience, I should become a coward. If I became a coward, I should never have the courage to face Gregory," she said, checking the points off on her fingers. "No, stop: I know what you're about to say, 'then you do mean some day to face Gregory.' I can't answer that, and you must be patient to let these ten days go by; maybe by the time we're in the middle of them I will have got back my wits. I'm too scared now to have any wits at all. What is going on in our house now? you know no more than I do, and yet you know just as I do that there is something strange. It's something between Silas and Gregory. Oh, it's dreadful to think that there should be something between them which they are working out for themselves, with all their difficulties, because they can't ask *our* help, either yours or mine. It frightens me so. Oh, my dear, it's horrible to be afraid! Linnet, you must take care of me."

"You don't give me much chance. . ."

"No, I know I don't; I'm bad to you, I know. I seem to turn this way and that for a way out, and things press upon me, and then I make you suffer for it. Put it down that I scarcely know what I'm doing. . ."

"No, I know you don't, my pretty, my poor pretty, only tell me about it, if that's any help, and don't let things get magnified in your mind bigger than they ought to be; hills look steeper than they are, you know, before one starts going up them."

"Oh," she said, her eyes brimming, "you're good and patient, indeed you are. I hardly understand, yet, what's come over us, that sometimes my breath comes short and I shut my eyes and think I must faint away with the longing to see you. I wish, sometimes I wish that something would happen—something quite outside this life, I mean,—to relieve us; I don't know what I mean, rightly. But it's the weight. . . and the longing. . . I can't keep still under it, at times; I have to get up and move about. . . the longing. . . the burning." She put her hand up to her throat as though she were physically oppressed. "And I put questions to myself—about you, I mean—and the answers come springing without my having to think. They leap out, the answers do. Would I die for you? Oh, so gladly! would I starve for you? yes, and never a word to let you know. Would I die if you died? I'd pine if I lived an hour after you'd gone. Would I give myself up to you? yes—to beat me if you chose; I'd shut my eyes and let you. . . That's love, isn't it? It's like striking a bell; it clangs back at once. And now—I can't help saying it—for ten days there'll be times when we're alone, and I'll be less starved than I am now; it seems I've just been keeping alive for this, and reach it all spent and gasping. Oh, nothing, nothing more! only to talk to you, and look at you; we're strangers still. I want to *drink* being with you. Then I'll be able to think, and we'll sort everything out, and get it clear. Only now I'm too parched for you, and too frightened of *them*. You must decide everything for me, and tell me what to do, and then take me away,—oh, take me away!"

She clung to him as she besought him, abandoning herself like a frightened child, and putting her arms up round his neck exactly like a child.

"My God, I didn't know you could speak so, or feel so. *I* felt so, but I didn't dare to tell you."

"I didn't know either. . . one doesn't know. . ." She had sunk so unrestrainedly against him, that but for his support she would have slipped down without resistance upon the floor. He felt that she would lie there, like a shot bird, at his feet, making no effort to rise, and letting her will glide away from her in a passive extinction of self; it would be for her the most exquisite, and at the same time the most spiritually voluptuous experience of her life. As it was, she had never known anything like the wild, fainting rapture of this half-surrender. "Linnet, Linnet," she said, pushing him away, "where are we? it won't do; we're being swept along; I'm afraid. Go right over there, to the other side of the room; no, farther away than that." She directed him with an imperious urgent finger. "You mustn't come any nearer. Promise. Sit down on that chair. I'll stop over here." She leant her head back against the wall.

"Now we couldn't well be farther apart," he said, having obeyed her. They were both pale as they looked at one another across the width of the room, and their breath came and went quickly between their parted lips.

"It's to be like this the whole time that Gregory is away. Then when he comes back I can tell him everything. If we had been different, I should tell him less easily."

Morgan was just able to follow the ethics of this argument.

"Now I'm going away," she continued; "you mustn't move. If you moved, I should run to you. . ."

"Oh, Nan!" he said, stretching out his hands to her across the room.

"No, no, no," she cried, vigorously shaking her head from side to side, the shake becoming more vigorous as her need for determination increased. "Oh, my darling heart," she cried, "I want so to come to you," and she fled from the room, leaving him unbalanced and perplexed, and in half a dozen minds as to whether he ought to submit as he did to her directions, or to take the law away from her by adopting a bolder course.

XIII

I

SHE LAY STILL ASLEEP IN her bed while Gregory prepared himself for his journey. He trod in stockinged feet upon the boards of the bedroom, throwing articles of clothing into a carpet bag, and stopping to glance at his wife who, with her hair loose on the pillow around her small face, looked like some fragile child, and like a child's too was the shape of her limbs beneath the thin covering of blanket. She lay sleeping; her lips parted. Gregory had purposely not roused her. It was her undoubted business to go downstairs, light the fire, and get him some breakfast, but he would forego the meal sooner than watch her moving about the house he was that day abandoning. He did not wish to carry away the picture of her at her familiar tasks, in which, he imagined, she would so soon be watched by another. In his fancy he pictured Morgan entering the house as soon as he, Gregory, had safely left it. Would they breakfast delightedly together? or would the fear of Silas counsel prudence? Again, as many times before, he was upon the point of renouncing his journey. He looked at Nan with his fists clinched, a storm of hatred and possession tearing him. His placid inward life, running as smoothly as the machines with which it was always occupied, had been disturbed lately, disturbed with a violence he would not have suspected; he was troubled and resentful, directing his resentment particularly against Nan who had brought this disturbance upon him. He glared at her as she lay asleep. He thought angrily that he should be allowed to live as a privileged designer of engines, not drawn into the fury of domestic calamity. His nature, once roused, held elements so harsh and intolerant, he knew, that it fitted him all too well for a part in such a calamity. Had he been aloof, indifferent. . . ah! how he coveted that gift of indifference. He had it not; he was too much of a Dene. So he dressed himself, packed his bag, and brooded resentment over Nan. She slept on; breathing softly; unconscious.

He was ready, but for his coat. He stood in his shirt sleeves looking at Nan and wondering whether he should wake her or slip away to the station with no farewell. Then he bent down and slid his arm beneath the pillow, lifting her bodily towards him. She woke with a cry, to find Gregory's face near hers as he knelt on the floor. It was very fortunate that he could not hear the cry, which, at first merely startled, changed to horror as she recognised him. His sardonic smile and her widened eyes were terribly close; their two faces, by reason of their nearness, seemed large to one another. She pushed with both hands against his chest, struggling silently; only half awake, she had not the wisdom not to struggle; now, she knew only his distastefulness. He held her, hardened to a cold fury by her resistance. He could see all her muscles exerted in the effort to get rid of him; even the corners of her mouth were drawn tight, and her eyes were fixed on him in concentration. She could not plead with him, as she could have with another man; their strife must be soundless; she pushed, and twisted herself within his grasp, both quite in vain, then, relaxing, she lay quiet, with his arm still beneath her. She stared up at him. She knew, and was terrified by, the expression in his eyes. He drew his hand from beneath her and sketched a rapid phrase on his fingers, at the same time moving towards her. She answered vehemently in the same manner, her arms pitifully slight and delicate as the loose nightgown fell back from them, and the fingers racing in gesticulation. His whole face darkened as he read; she saw that an angry obstinacy was taking possession of him. She tried to escape from the opposite side of her bed, but he seized her again, holding her down, determined, revengeful, and unshaken by pity. She sought wildly in her mind for some means of release, finding none, when she heard Calthorpe's voice calling for Gregory beneath the window.

II

SHE WAS SAVED, HE HAD gone, flinging on his coat and snatching his carpet-bag, but for long she remained trembling and fearing his return. She shuddered at intervals as she remembered their struggle, conducted in that horrible silence; their antagonism had been so condensed; none of it could slip away in words. She could still feel where his fingers had gripped into her flesh. If Calthorpe had not come! Now, now, they were on the road to Spalding; she was alone in the house, she was to breakfast with Silas and Linnet. Her shudders of horror gave place to the sweet shivering she knew when she thought of Linnet, an etherealised desire, a trembling of her spirit more than of her body, a going out towards a young and fit companion, who by a refinement of perfection was also a lover. Gradually she ceased to think of Gregory, and lost herself in the other thought, lying propped up on her pillow with an unconscious smile of heavenly happiness in her eyes and upon her lips. She rose presently, and in the same dream started to dress, delighting in the touch of the cold water she splashed over her throat and arms. The puritanical neatness of each garment, and the fibre of her laundered linen, likewise satisfied her as she became clothed. She had noticed how, without any exaggeration of fancy, small physical experiences were intensified of late,—colours were brighter, the song of birds more ringing, her flesh more sensitive to the touch, and in looking at people she had observed how the pores of their skin were distinct, or the firm planting of eyelashes, and sweep of eyebrow,—all these things, that were foolishly unimportant, but that added a vividness to daily life. She was in every detail more keenly alive; her nostrils dilated to smell the air, and she touched the sill of the window, where the wood was faintly warm under the sun, with a sense of comradeship. She moved, too, with a difference; her tread became resilient; her foot was springy as it poised upon the ground. Her small head carried itself with a light elasticity in the air, and she was actually conscious of the soft mass of her hair that caressed the nape of her neck as she turned her head. She had a wish for woods and cornlands; to sit in the roots of a tree beside a brook, allowing the water to eddy between her staying fingers; to bathe her body in a lake or in the surf of the sea. So, in loving one man, one loved the whole company of earth? Love was illimitable indeed, if it conferred that privilege, a wider thing than mere absorption in a fellow-being that was a creature, after all, of limitations as narrow as any other.

III

THEY WERE ALONE, THE THREE of them, the absence of Gregory so startlingly unprecedented that despite Silas's presence she obtained a foretaste of complete and sudden solitude with Linnet. She was admitted, she, the starved, to a feast of dominion. She found herself translated into a world where she, most marvellously, was the object of reverence and solicitude, and under this warmth of spoiling her natural grace expanded even beyond the anticipation of his delight. Aware that those ten days were but a reprieve, she gave herself up to making the most of them,—in so far as was consistent with the narrow rulings of her conscience. Linnet, exasperated at times, but ruefully submissive always, acknowledged and obeyed her imperious orders. She was very happy in her control of him; all the happier, perhaps in the knowledge that she owed it solely to the consent of his chivalry, without which (O, exquisite danger!) her security would, like glass, be shivered.

There was, unforgettably, Silas. Silas proclaiming himself a friend, but, nevertheless, remaining a spy, a jailer. Silas who seemed to come upon them with a queer noiselessness; who cried, "Well?" over their shoulders, and who then, suddenly swooping down upon them, swept with his hands to learn whether they were sitting close together, or apart. They were always apart. Angered, he would say, "Well?" again, this time with a forced benevolence in his voice; and sometimes he would amuse himself by walking along between them, hilarious, taking an arm of each. This method of surprising them, this sham benevolence, this reasonless hilarity, struck cold terror into Nan as something indefinably sinister. Once, too, when she met Silas tapping his way over the cobbles towards the letter-box, on the envelope which he carried in his hand she read the name and address of Gregory. (Silas had adapted with delight this method of communication. He rubbed his hands together when he thought of Gregory, in Birmingham, tearing the flap open and scanning the lines of those able, indefinite letters.) But at other times she was puzzled by the hungry interest with which he questioned her, and in which her ear did not detect the usual unalloyed malignity, but rather a wistfulness, a desire to be admitted to a lovely secret, a genuine craving for participation, however humble, however incomplete, and beggarly upon the fringe of riches. At such times an eagerness crept into his face, as he bent forward to question her, his hands hanging loosely interlaced between his knees, the strong cords of his throat standing out in sculptural masses of light and shadow; words came from him almost timidly, as though he feared to presume or to give offence, but must nevertheless urge his examination, irresistibly tempted and allured. Nan, who sat sewing, looked into his face with wonderment. Experience taught her mistrust, but instinct taught her a heart-searching pity. There was always that same feeling which she had for Silas, which she could not explain, and which nothing,—no dread, no premonition, no knowledge,—could permanently destroy. It reawakened always at the sound of his yearning voice. Once it led her to put her fingers on his forehead, "How much you've missed!"

He sprang away, detected at the very moment when forgetful absorption had suspended his defiance.

"I've had all I wanted. Make no mistake. You're wasting your sloppy pity. . ."

IV

GREGORY HAD BEEN SO SUDDENLY and so completely withdrawn! She adapted herself without bewilderment to the new order. She became as a girl, betrothed to Linnet. Their relationship had all the innocence of a betrothal. Her past life might have been blotted out, the future so far distant (down a vista of ten days!) as to be, for all practical purposes, negligible. She could have drawn from this a proof that the violence of the years lived between Gregory and Silas had made upon her being only a mark such as might be soon effaced. She, the true Nan, had slipped away from violence, because violence was so unalterably alien to her. The lesson of violence was a lesson she might provisionally learn, but would never long remember. She went out now to meet the condition she had always wanted: the secure tenderness, the settlement, once and for all, in her choice; she was not one who would demand variety upon the face of existence. Variety! she had had it; excitement, uncertainty, passion, and the weight of failure all around her, reckless because resigned; she had had all that, compressed within the limits of an iron circle; those were not the things she wanted. The things she wanted were the things that Linnet could give her.

The subtle sarcasms of Silas were incapable of troubling her quiet discernment.

XIV

I

THEIR LAST AFTERNOON, A SATURDAY. They believed that Gregory was to return at seven; only Silas knew that he was to return at five. With the hoarding instinct that this knowledge might be useful to him, he kept it a secret. They were very silent, and remained close to one another, holding hands. How grave they were! They were very self-contained, husbanding all their strength. He knew that they meant to beard Gregory that evening, but he, Silas, equally, meant to outwit them, and he thought with satisfaction that his cunning was greater than theirs. He considered their silence with an irony more tragic than any of them knew. The pain that their company had cost him during the last ten days; the pain, too, which his own desire for their happiness had cost him; his angry, resentful love for them both; the strain of remaining true to his principles, and his vindictiveness (Christine! Christine! always Christine, recurrent, gnawing), all this mingled in his mind to a state of folly with which he was almost unable prudently to deal. He acknowledged that he had been partly to blame. He had drawn out Nan's confidences. But his temperament inclined him harshly towards self-flagellation. . .

"Only a little time now, Nan, before he's here," he said. "You'll have much to tell him, much that'll interest him. Remember, if you want any help, I'm here: Silas is here. Him being my brother, we understand one another, like you and Linnet understand one another. Blood brothers is close like lovers. Close as lovers.—But what call have I to talk of love, seeing I never knew it, nor wanted it?"

He went outside and sat on the doorstep, leaning his back against the closed door. The village street was deserted, distant voices sounded from the green; in the faint warmth of the April sun the paint of the door smelt hot, and flies buzzed stickily in the corners of the woodwork. Silas sat there clasping his knees, and swaying slightly to the ironical rhythm of his own thoughts. He felt like a jailer, keeping those two imprisoned inside; they were happy, in spite of the imminent crisis; merely and childishly happy because they were together,—that sufficed; he had learnt during those ten days the perfection of their happiness. Nan had betrayed, under his questionings, more than she had probably intended to betray, and under the pain of defrauded envy he had accumulated a store of knowledge. They seemed to *be* one another; it was not so much sympathy that they enjoyed, as identity. Silas swayed himself slowly backwards and forwards; he put the tip of his tongue between his teeth and held it there; he tapped his boots softly together because of his enjoyment. They were inside, talking; Gregory would be home soon. It tickled Silas's fancy to think he had a surprise up his sleeve in store for them; he, the unwanted third! he, the ostracised of the village! they would soon learn, all of them, that he still had fangs. He strained his ears to catch the first sound of the train, which, after stopping at Spalding, crossed the fenny country at some little distance. He wished for the dulled rumble indicative that the train was upon its journey and therefore that Gregory and Calthorpe were upon their way to Abbot's Etchery along the dyke, but at the same time he wished this hour prolonged, an hour so entirely after his own heart. He had so many revenges to take, so many old debts to wipe off, that no luxury of procrastination could be too great. Provided only, indeed, that the completion was sufficient, and sufficiently inevitable; and as to this he had no misgivings.

He never heard the train. He continued to hear only the distant shouts from the green, the small noises of insects, and the murmur within the room—not a continued murmur, only an intermittent one— and the first sound that drew him from his torpor of satisfaction was that of footsteps on the cobbles and Calthorpe's voice, in its somewhat irritatingly cheery tones, "Friend Silas! well, I've brought back Gregory safe and sound, and how are you all at home?"

Gregory stood planted in the middle of the street watching his brother's face for his greeting of Calthorpe. His throat heaved, and his suppressed violence, which was entirely apparent, made his stiff black travelling suit and bowler hat seem puerile and ridiculous. He was in one of those primitive moods when civilised trappings become laughable: an angry man in a bowler hat. . . Not only angry, but convulsed with anxiety, and with a rage that prayed only to be released. Yes, even though that rage must destroy his soul, it craved for an outlet. A man so minded would not have thanked the reassuring speech that drove back the straining rage as unwarrantable. The bag he carried was as paper in his hand. His limbs seemed to burst out of his clothes; strong muscle impatient for nakedness. His throat reared itself out of his collar. His hands protruded starkly from his cuffs. Civilisation upon him was as preposterous as the naked man wrestling beneath was superb. He stood with his feet planted wide apart, in the attitude of one who awaits and encourages an attack.

Silas was petulant at being taken by surprise; "I didn't expect you," he said, as though he had been cheated of his due. "Well, now that we're here, let us come in," said Calthorpe, still good-humoured, but slightly uneasy; he would have liked the numbers increased, not fancying the part of sole interpreter between the brothers; was he to act as light to the one, and as sound to the other? The constant companionship of Gregory, and, above all, the railway journey that day, and the walk along the dyke, had convinced him that all was very far from well amongst the Denes. "No," said Silas, standing up and stretching his arms crucifix-wise across the door, "you can't go in there."

Gregory saw the gesture, which was intelligible enough, although he did not hear the words. A perverse relief swept over him, at having his worst dread confirmed. A horrible inarticulate noise broke from him, which made Calthorpe swing round in his direction. "Good God," said Calthorpe appalled, "it's like a baboon," and he continued to stare, expecting the noise to be repeated. Silas, too, had heard; "Yes—like a brute," he said, becoming transfigured with delight as he saw the certainty of manœuvring that brute with the cunning of his own intellect. Gregory never uttered a sound unless he was extraordinarily moved. "Tell him, Mr. Calthorpe," said Silas, "that he can't go into my cottage."

"He wants to know why," said Calthorpe, having delivered this message and received the answer from Gregory's quivering fingers. "He looks as though he might spring upon you at any moment, Silas." He watched, anxiously, first one and then the other.

"Gathering himself together, is he?"

"Yes—he doesn't look as though he'd hold himself in much longer. Oh, you wouldn't chuckle if you could see him."

"Tell him to trust me and not to be a fool."

"He says, was it true?"

"Tell him first, that he must let me manage things."

"I don't like the look of this, Silas; I'm all in the dark."

"Never mind, sir; you just tell him to trust me."

"He'll be at your throat if I don't," and the communication passed silently from Calthorpe to Gregory. "He says he will trust you a bit longer, but he wants to see things for himself."

Silas appeared to be perplexed by his brother's impatience, and by the danger of Calthorpe putting two and two together.

"Ask him if he will wait till tomorrow," he said, at length.

This suggestion so enraged Gregory that he leapt at his brother and was only warded off by Calthorpe's appeasing gesture. He fell back a pace, and framed a message with shaking hands.

"He says," said Calthorpe, "that he will be damned if he waits another five minutes. And I am damned myself, Silas," added the honest instrument, "if I understand a word of this, or if I will go on letting you make a cat's-paw of me for your black tricks. Call Mrs. Dene, who perhaps knows what you are up to."

Silas was outwardly calm, but alert. He must lose no time in breaking up the trio.

"I shall explain everything to you, Mr. Calthorpe," he said earnestly, still standing with his arms flung wide across the door, "but he's a dangerous man, my brother. He's in a dangerous temper. To tell you the truth, Mr. Calthorpe," he ran on with extreme glibness, "he suspects someone of tampering with his designs—but keep that for yourself. I've got the proofs inside my cottage, only I didn't expect you so early. We must get him away. Tell him to go into his own place and change his clothes, and I'll send his wife to him."

"Well, there seems to be no harm in that," said Calthorpe dubiously.

"Believe me, sir, I'm acting for the best."

"H'm—you seem mighty eager to get your brother out of the way."

"Surely you only have to look at him, Mr. Calthorpe."

Calthorpe looked, and, having done so, he asked Gregory to go. "But I am damned if I understand," he said again, taking off his hat and scratching his head. "You Denes are hard fellows to make out," he added in an access of irritation, seeing the expression on Silas's face, and indeed he felt that his irritation was only small and petulant beside the anger of Gregory and the sardonic malevolence of Silas. If it were not for Nan, he would wash his hands of the whole lot of them. His easy-going philosophy of life was too greatly disturbed by the stress and inexplicable ferment of the Denes. He saw Gregory scowling in his indecision, than a message came from the able fingers, which he passed on to Silas. "He says he will wait for his wife in his own cottage."

"Tell him she shall join him there," said Silas grimly.

II

DEVASTATION MET NAN'S EYES WHEN she hurried into her cottage. The white lace curtains were torn from the windows and the pictures lay

V. SACKVILLE-WEST

scattered about the floor. Any ornament or attempt at decoration had been snatched from its place and flung across the room. In the midst of this wreckage stood Gregory, in his shirt sleeves, his chest heaving and his bronze forehead shining with sweat. He held out to Nan a paper upon which he had written, "*Plain deel tables and chairs is good enough for us, without fal-lals.*" She read it, and with tears running over her cheeks knelt down to gather up her broken china, collecting the pieces tenderly into the shreds of the curtains. Gregory came towards her and kicked the things away from her hand. She knelt upon the floor, gazing up at him without protest but with inexpressible sorrow. Everytime she renewed her gesture of gathering up the shares, he scattered them again by a kick, until in discouragement she desisted, waiting for his next manifestation. She dared not get up while he stood over her in his threatening attitude.

Silas came in; Nan found herself turning to him as towards a friend. Here, at least, was one who had some influence over Gregory! She felt herself the alien before the brothers.

Silas was sympathetic. Silas commiserated. Let her go away for a little, and he would soothe Gregory. Gregory had behaved like a peevish child. He, Silas, would remonstrate. He even patted Nan's shoulder kindly as she passed him, drying her eyes, to leave the brothers together as she was bid.

XV

I

IT WAS NOT LONG BEFORE she returned, and saw Silas alone, with the wreckage created by Gregory's rage still around him.

"Silas!" she exclaimed, going up to him, "where's Gregory?—where's Linnet?"

"You ask for them in the same breath?" he replied.

"But I must know!" she said, catching hold of his arm and peering urgently into his face. "Silas, what dreadful excitement is making you so quiet, so strung-up like? Don't think that I can't see it. You're gathered all into yourself, like as though you were waiting, and your face looks so strange. Silas! you are in a trance? For pity's sake, speak to me. If you won't speak, I must go. I can't stop here. I'm going out—to look for them both. Only, if you can tell me aught, won't you do so, Silas? you could if you would, I'm sure, and I'm so broken by terror, Silas, if you can help me now you'll surely not refuse?"

"The sinner must expect to pay," he said slowly, his eyes wide open and glazed into impassivity.

"But I haven't sinned, God be my judge!" she cried, wringing her hands together. "Silas, I do conjure you, as you hope for mercy yourself, let your lips speak; tell me—for you know—where they've gone, and why? Tell me where I can find them. Oh, if I were there, I could come between them, and if Gregory must injure me, why, then, he must, but I should *know*, I should know; it's this doubt, this knowing that they're together, this not knowing what they may be saying! it kills me, Silas. Silas, see here, listen to me, Silas: I've not been bad to you, have I, Silas? We've not been bad to you, Linnet and I? Well, have a little mercy on us now: we've loved, yes, but we've done no more wrong than that. I wouldn't, with Gregory away. We were to tell Gregory everything, so soon as he came back. You know that, Silas.—Oh, you'll not help me: I see it by your face. What are you thinking of? I never saw you look so terrible. But I haven't time to beseech you more; I must go, and take my chance of finding them, and may your wicked heart be afraid for whatever goes amiss."

"You'll not go," he said suddenly, holding her down.

She struggled against him.

"Silas, you hurt my wrist; let go, I say. Oh, I see it: you're in with Gregory, you've tricked us; my God, what can Linnet and I do against you and Gregory?—You laugh at that, you fiend," she said, quietening into despair; "you laugh," she said, rocking her head piteously from side to side, "you laugh, you laugh!"

"Gregory's honest," he pronounced; "I've got three of you, not two, in the net. Gregory's my dupe too; he's an honest man."

"But, then, why? in God's name, *why*? what is it, Silas? are you mad or sane? Are we to be your toys? What have we done to you? What had Hannah done?"

"Hannah? . . ."

"You killed Hannah."

He still held her down on a chair, and by the high standard of their present stress the retrospective admission that he had killed Hannah seemed to them both subordinate. He was breathing heavily.

"Hannah laughed at me and fooled me; she was rough with me, and sweet-tongued enough with other men. I wasn't going to be fooled by Hannah. She'd thrown in her lot with mine, and if I suffered she should suffer too. That's why I killed Hannah. The world's been made black for me; I'll make it black for others."

"It's awful, your revengefulness. . . But I tried to make it *less* black, Silas, so did Linnet; look, I don't ask you now to help me, or to tell me anything, but only to let me go,—won't you, Silas? It's so easy for you to keep me here; I can't escape from your strength if you're determined to hold me. But I beg you; I beseech you. Often you tried me high, and if I failed you I ask your forgiveness. Only let me go now. Don't *help* me; I don't ask that; only give me the chance of helping myself. I ask with all the patience and humbleness in me; I'm in bitter anguish, Silas. Gregory's hard enough, Heaven knows, but he's got the heart of a woman next to you."

"Gregory's less bereft than I; I only have my own mind to feed upon."

"Surely that's true of us all, blind or not blind?" she said, in a weak attempt at argument.

"Then I was born with a darkened mind, not only with darkened eyes," he exclaimed violently, and with renewed determination. "I'm cursed with the one as much as with the other, and though God knows no justice I'll throw in my quota to balance the scales: I never deserved the curse I got, but, since I got it, I'll deserve it; and I'll see to it that others get something they don't deserve, as I did myself. Did you ever consider what blindness meant? To be dependent on others' charity, to be a burden, a maimed thing? above all to have to submit to pity, when you were born with a spirit that wanted the *envy* of other men?"

"Silas, Silas, all that's just words, and meantime you're draining the life out of me."

"You're not Nan," he said, "not Nancy Dene; you're just the victim of *my* curse. What does it matter that you never knew Lady Malleson? Blind, you call me? why, I think we're all blind—blind instruments, not more blind one than the other."

"Gregory only breaks my things," she cried out, kicking with her toe at a fragment of china, "but you're putting all my happiness in pieces."

"Yes," said Silas, "I told you he was an honest man."

"That's why we would have put everything to him honestly," she began with extreme earnestness; "we would have told him we hadn't sought one another out, but that something led us. . . We had talked it all over, what we would say. Silas, will nothing soften you? You talk about courage: we meant to be brave, not deceitful; you even urged us, once, after the fire, to hold to one another if we loved truly. You said we were the builders; you talked beautiful. I never knew a man talk like you talk, sometimes, Silas. You seem all lifted-up. . . Maybe you wouldn't see so bright if you didn't see so black. I had a feeling for you; oh yes, I had! Though all the while I knew about Hannah, and after Hannah, Martin. But I didn't know then that after Hannah and Martin it would be me and Linnet—and Linnet! You seemed kindly to us, of late. Was it *all* a trap? did you never *feel* kindly while you spoke us fair? Oh, Silas, everything's going from me. It'll go badly between Linnet and Gregory. If I was there, I'd manage; you fight things as they come along; and Linnet, he needs me to look after him. He'll be stiff and buttoned-up with Gregory, but that's not the worst: it's Gregory I'm afraid of. Not speaking, he puts everything into his fists; you know what he's like, Silas. And Linnet's my life,—my life. I'm telling you more than I ever told him, save once. Won't you let me go?" She moved her wrist tentatively within the clench of his fingers.

"I waste, I fail," said Silas, holding her wrist more closely than before; "the day you came from Sussex to Abbot's Etchery you were meant to fall in with me. I told you already, you're not Nan Dene; you're a thing. You're part of my design. You, and your little loves, and dreams and what-not—I'll *grind* you. When I was a boy, I set out to give people as bad a time as I had myself. My mother hated my father and was afraid of him; he used to jeer at her when he saw how much she hated

Gregory and me. Because we were deformed, you understand. Once I was given a rabbit for a pet; well, I put out its eyes with a needle. That makes you shiver: I hold that it was only just. Now I've got you; you'll be better game than Hannah, because that was over too quickly; but you, once Linnet is taken away from you, and you're brought back where you belong, to my brother, to be my brother's wife, his faithful, broken, submissive wife—I'll know that everyday your prettiness will wither, you'll never sing, you'll never put out china for Gregory to break, you'll shun young men because you'll have known the pain of love, you'll bury your heart below a mound, and your hopes beside your heart, and so you'll grow old between Gregory and me, and we'll speak less and less, until you and I sit as silent as Gregory himself."

He paused, but she gave only a small moan.

"You were right," he went on, "Linnet is with Gregory now. I sent Linnet off, and now I've sent Gregory to join him. You won't see him again,—not if I know Gregory. Gregory won't tell us what took place between them,—not he! He'll come home presently, and you'll get our supper, and have yours between us, and after supper Gregory'll get out his drawings. And every evening afterwards will be the same,—exactly the same. Maybe you'll have children and watch them growing like me; you don't know, yet, what seeds might be lying in your children's minds. I'd watch over them, never fear; I'll not have my nephews grow into milksops, into sentimental dabs. . ."

He spoke with such virulence that Nan cried out, unbearably slashed. That seemed to gratify him, for he settled down into an intermittent growl:—

"Your children.—Your sons.—But Denes, all the same.—Who stands alone?" he muttered, taken up on that revived train of thought, "Who stands single? no one, it seems; your sons wouldn't be solely yours. Where's independence? not in this world. O folly! to let it slide, even in part, into another's keeping. Where would be your trouble now, if Linnet hadn't your heart? Freedom goes when the heart goes.—Not strong enough.—Loneliness and labour,—yes, surely."

"'Tisn't all that, 'tis happiness you grudge," said Nan, suddenly bitter.

"That's your little view: there spoke Nan Dene!—And if you thought that, anyway why did you flaunt your happiness in my face? Eh?"

"Oh, Silas, you kept asking me. . ."

"And if I did! Was it part of your kindness that you boast of, to give me the glimpse of a feast I couldn't share? Was it meant as a treat? You'd be willing to give me kindness; I couldn't expect more,—a blind man like me. Very lucky to get as much." He roared suddenly with laughter. "That's a pallid sort of thing to offer,—I won't give you thanks for that," he cried.

Nan thought that he was really going mad; madness and disaster had broken crashing over her world. The forces loosed were too great and too bewildering for her to strive against; the sanity of Linnet, the sanity of their joy, was lost forever, lost, foundered in the madness of the hurricane brought about by Silas and Gregory. For Gregory there might be some excuse; Silas appeared to be possessed by a senseless, impersonal fury of destruction. She thought she might as well argue with the unleashed elements as with Silas in his bitterness and diabolical delight. Yet life still moved, still endeavoured; and, pricked by its promptings, she struggled,—

"You hurt me and Linnet because we are safe to hurt; we can't hurt you back."

"It's not true!" he yelled.

She was utterly astonished at the effect she had produced.

"But, Silas," she said, inspired, "we all know you for a coward. We all know your talk for bluster. Did you think we didn't know that, by now?"

II

SHE HAD NOT AT FIRST spoken tauntingly. She thought she had meant only to pronounce the truth. Then she perceived that the truth had cut deeper than any taunt. She was as a naked, unarmed person driven up against a wall, that finds suddenly a blade put into their hands. She held it, but was perplexed how best to use it. She made a thrust,—

"All your talk is talk. It costs you nothing to ruin Linnet and me. It cost you nothing to throw out Martin.—And Hannah," she whispered, "and Hannah!—What have you ever done that hurt yourself?"

From the tremor of the hand still clutching her wrist she discovered that he was shuddering.

"You dare speak to me so?" he threatened.

"Hit me,—I can't hit back," she replied, upheld.

But he made no movement to injure her. His defeat was as complete as it was sudden. Against his determination, which no appeal could have moved, no bribe impressed, she had turned the sole effective weapon, his own intrinsic weakness. There was no repair possible to a breach that had started from the inside. She had struck down upon the rot within him and the inner walls of his defences crumbled.

III

FAILING TO UNDERSTAND WHAT SHE had brought about, she sat watching him, alarmed, perplexed, but, through her confusion, something stirred, which might perhaps not be called hope, but which was at least removed from the despondency of death that had lately descended upon her. He maintained upon her wrist a grasp that had now become automatic; he sat bent, covering his eyes with his free hand. She recognised only that he must work his way towards his decision without interference on her part; he was beyond such interference, and although the stealing away of time roused her anxiety to the pitch of physical pain, she constrained herself to wait, tense, in the knowledge that Silas passed through a crisis no less momentous than her own. He moved his body uneasily about, and unintelligible mumblings like groans escaped him. He fought; he wrestled. He fixed that sightless gaze upon Nan, saying in tones of reluctant abnegation, "And am I to end so?" He cried out once, startling her by the anguish that tore his voice, "Failure! failure! beaten by a jeer! weakness beats me; poor blind Silas, poor weak Silas, couldn't stick to his purpose even when his end was in sight!" One thing was clear, that he suffered intensely; but the complexity of his sufferings was hopelessly beyond her comprehension. She could only wait, and, trembling, watch. She no longer tried to free her wrist, fearing by that mere flutter of self-assertion to recall his former mood. She tried to pray, and her mind produced a prayer like a child's, "Please, God. . ." His ravings had ceased, and nothing now came from him but the small phrases that jerked themselves to the surface, after which the riot and despair of his thoughts were again submerged. "Flotsam and jetsam," he muttered. Striking his chest, he said, "Here stands Silas Dene, who helped two children to happiness,—let that be my epitaph!" "Where's truth? do I know my own mind, or don't I?" After these disjointed remarks, that emerged at intervals, like milestones marking off the painful road he was travelling, he released her and stood up. "I'll save you yet," he pronounced. "Stay you there and let me manage things my own way. You've nothing to fear now,—once there was something to fear in me, perhaps, but that's a thing of the past. That's finished. You stay where you are, and I'll bring Linnet to you."

"You may be too late," she said.

"I'm not too late," he replied, with such certainty that she was misled into thinking he had some inner knowledge.

He put her quite gently away from him as she tried to detain him, pleading to be allowed to help.

IV

HE PASSED OUT OF THE house, guiding himself by his finger-tips that brushed lightly against the doorpost. Not daring to disobey by following him, Nan saw him thus lower himself to the doorstep, whence he set out down the street in the direction of the factory, slipping his fingers along the walls of the houses. She wondered whether she might venture to follow at a distance. Inactivity seemed, in that pregnant hour, intolerable.—Slowly she put her shawl over her head and stood in the doorway holding the edges of the shawl close under her chin, and exerting her eyes to keep pace with Silas. He strode on as though confident in perfect vision; only that outstretched hand slipping rapidly from house to house set any peculiar mark upon his progress. But Nan, with a solicitude whose almost maternal quality she recognised with a shock of dismay, thought, "He's going much too fast," for she made no allowance for the quickening of all his instincts under the exalted condition of his mind. She had now no enmity towards him. She was too well-used to his violence to bear him any grudge for that, and moreover, in her eyes, if he intervened on her behalf and Linnet's, he was redeemed. She recognised obscurely that he had considered himself shamed,—shamed to the extent of catastrophe—but this problem she banished as beyond the scope of her understanding. If he would but come to her aid and Linnet's she would accept,—oh, with what thankfulness!—the benefit at his hands without perplexity or investigation.

He had turned the corner, and, keeping her distance, she began to follow.

V

WHEN THE FACTORY CAME IN sight she realised from the absence of movement about the buildings, that six o'clock had long since struck and that the work-people, in consequence, had left their employment for the day. The evening shift, reduced to a minimum, would be occupied in one or two specialised portions only,—in the boiler-rooms, for example, or amongst the engines. For all practical purposes the Denes had the place to themselves. A terrible doubt overcame her: might Silas, still, be playing the double game? She pressed onward, dwarfed by the immense sheds and chimneys that bulked around her. She could see Silas as he crossed the tessellated square. He advanced with scarce more caution, although he had now no wall to guide him, and, having no stick, held his hand at arm's length before him until some contact should bring him up short. She had the dread that, did he but turn round, he would perceive her. She walked on tiptoe, skirting the sheds under cover of the great water-butts. Sick terror possessed her, and the imminence of disaster weighed her down.

She saw Silas reach the foot of the long, outside, ladder-like stairs that led to the upper gallery of the main building, and, setting his feet confidently upon the iron steps, begin to climb.

VI

He climbed without pause, dwindling to a small figure aloft, to Nan so far below. She leant in collapse against a huge tarred water-butt, pitiably undecided whether by ascending after him she would do more harm or good. The question was of such importance to her, but its resolution depended upon her poor unguided wisdom, and she shrank from the responsibility. Still Silas climbed, and stood at last upon the topmost landing, and disappeared from her view.

When he disappeared she hesitated no longer, but ran from her shelter of concealment, and started pulling herself up on the ascent. She went up the steep stairs, pulling hand over hand on the iron rail that served on one side as banister. She thought that she would soon be on a level with the black smoke floating from the chimneys. Through the perforations of the iron steps she could see the ground below, and when she turned her head she found that the roofs of the village had become apparent. She had never been up this way before, but always by the inner staircase. But Silas, of course, had chosen the more gaunt, the more perilous method of approach.

Landings on the way up admitted to two other storeys; these she passed, having a glimpse of machinery within. The top windows, square and bleak, were those of the gallery,—Gregory's gallery. She was upon the landing, and slipped in through the door which had been left ajar. Everything moved quickly now, too quickly to admit of any interference or direction, and what would be done now would never have the chance of being undone, nor would there be time for any reckoning or dexterity, in the vehemence of colliding passions that listened to no argument and were endowed with a strength beyond the reasoned energy of will.

Inside the five-hundred foot length of gallery the vats stretched away in low regular ranks, under the even light of the flat windows, pale-brown with dirt. The soap in the vats shifted and breathed; spat and slithered as it boiled. Linnet lay unconscious on the ground, as though he had been dropped there by a man surprised at his work; cast down with no more care than a toy by some formidable strength; and forgetful of prudence, Nan was instantly on her knees beside him. The other two were at a little distance, obvious of all save their last terrible combat. Speech and sight respectively denied them, a finer understanding taught them mutual penetration. They might have been ringed about by flames. They were alert only for one another. Kneeling on the ground at Linnet's side, Nan kept her gaze fastened upon them: it was to her very strange that Gregory should appear so fully aware of his brother's change of front. That he was aware of it, there could be no doubt; he had set himself ready in the attitude of a wrestler awaiting an onslaught. And Silas,—had heaven miraculously restored sight to Silas, that he advanced with such slow certainty towards his brother? He crouched, stalking him. He never once blundered against a vat.

Gregory leapt suddenly upon him, and in an instant their limbs were locked.

VII

THUS GRAPPLED, THEY SEEMED TO sway as a double monster heroically proportioned, a Herculean group against the flat light of the pale-brown windows. So superbly matched were they in physique that they remained almost motionless, swaying very slightly and with difficulty under the strain of their utmost effort. That stillness and that silence accompanying so supreme a struggle, were startling, portentous, and unnaturally impressive, as though the contained violence within were too mighty, too self-sufficient, to seek the relief of any visible outlet whether of noise or movement. Their meeting was a muffled encounter of force with force; it had not the crash of a collision. So they remained, arrested, stirred only by that almost imperceptible rocking, until doubt might have arisen whether they so held one another grasped with deadly intent, or, as the likeness between them more palpably emerged, in a brotherly welding against some danger imminent and extraneous. Their feet yielded not at all from their original planting upon the boards, their arms flung around one another had neither relaxed nor shifted, the slight angle at which their bodies were bent remained the same. The group they formed was of bronze beneath the spanning iron girders. But indeed the question became one of endurance, while the body's tension, flung on the hollowed hips, the quivering thighs, the knotted calves, and lean ankles, strained and cracked under the sustained tautening of human sinew. The one who was first to yield, by so much as the stagger of a foot, would find the advantage narrowly pursued, his opponent weighing down upon him, pressing him hard across their meagre margin.—Yet, were they meeting in alliance or hostility, the two brothers, so alike in their carved features, in the duplication of torso and huge opposing members?

Very slowly they bent together, straining; very slowly straightened themselves again to their formation of deadlock. All this strife took place without a sound, and seemed to occupy a long period of time, as though that group were permanent in the gallery, taking on the dingy monochrome and adapting itself to the proportions of the gallery's enormous setting. Nan, the impotent onlooker, could foresee no ending, no outcome. She saw that Gregory stared into his brother's face with a concentration of hatred. There was very little to indicate the intense pressure of strength that each was putting forth. But a difference was creeping in,—certainly a difference was creeping in. Gregory's determination was becoming the determination of misgiving, Silas's that of ultimate mastery. He did not appear triumphant, but quietly sure. Throughout, he had been guided by that security of vouchsafed insight.

Nan dared not stir. She continued to kneel beside Linnet, who still lay with his eyes closed, and the mark of a bruise blackening rapidly on his temple. She was deeply thankful for his unconsciousness.

The other two held her eyes. Gregory shifted a foot backwards to steady his balance; it was their first definite movement. Their faces were close; not angry, but concentrated, and Silas's was like a cast mask of unflinching patience. It frightened Nan to look at Silas's face, he was so immeasurably beyond both the greatness and the smallness of things human. He was like an incarnation of purpose, summoned for one set, finite task. His pressure was beginning to tell upon Gregory, who sought to improve his grip, but lost ground in so doing, and, staggering backwards, was driven to prop himself against the side of a vat. Here their grapple became more desperate, more final, in the same unbroken silence. Nan's imagination could not extend to reasons or to outcome; it did not extend beyond the struggle of the moment. She was numbed; all energy was absorbed by that group of wrestling Titans.

She bent down to Linnet, whose eyes had opened dazedly upon her. When she looked up again she saw a change. Silas had stooped until his arms clasped his brother below the waist. For one terrible moment she saw Gregory lifted off his feet, his arms flung impotently up, his body bent back in its supreme effort, his throat extended, to give vent to the most hideous sound she had ever heard uttered. Silas bore him up for a moment in that gesture of appalling ravishment, rearing like a centaur in the full magnificence of his strength; and with one mighty heave cast the burden from him into the boiling yellow slime of the vat.

XVI

I

NAN ROSE UPRIGHT, CRYING ALOUD; the wind of terror had blown violently in upon the stillness of the gallery. Silas towered amongst the vats; he wore an air of unearthly triumph and exaltation. "Nan! Nan!" he said, stretching up both arms with the gesture of the fanatic over the blood-offering. "What have you done? what have you done?" she cried. "Saved you,—bought you free," he answered loudly, still lit up by his triumph, but she hid her face in her hands, and moaned, shuddering.

Morgan stirred, and lay gazing without comprehension. He whispered Nan's name; she started, and turned to him, but seeing his eyes opened she wildly laid her hand across them. "You mustn't look,—you mustn't look," she said, distraught, in the effort to preserve him although she understood nothing herself.

In that absence of understanding she saw only Silas erect there with his arms still stretched out, as a sinner might stare into heaven, or a martyr into hell, accepting either, because enlightened as to both.

"Silas!" she called, unbearably alarmed.

"Builders and destroyers," he replied from afar, and in the tone of one giving utterance to a quotation of secret familiarity.

"What am I to do?" she cried, in a lost whisper. She felt immeasurably removed from the succour of mankind, forced into the kindred of the Denes, amongst grotesque surroundings, and grotesque and terrible events, high above the comings and goings of the temperate world. There was no room in her mind for the thought that the body of Gregory was pitched sinking through the morass of that deadly cauldron. Then the word "Gregory!" came to her, and, wonderingly, she pronounced it aloud, "Gregory," thereby bringing realisation upon herself, and the first conscious dismay.

She went to Silas and seized him by the arm.

"Silas, speak to me. . ."

He turned his eyes full upon her face.

"O God, can you *see* me?" she murmured, shrinking away.

"There was nothing else to be done," he said.

"Oh, yes, yes!" she protested, inarticulate in her extreme distress and bewilderment.

"There was nothing else," he repeated.

II

SHE PERCEIVED THEN THAT, ACCORDING to the temper of his mind, there was indeed nothing else. She ceased to protest, overtaken by the actual consequence of his uncompromising creed.

"You have killed Gregory," she said.

A change came over him; his look of flaming justification died down. "Hannah. Martin. Christine. Gregory," he said sorrowfully.

Nan was crying; she was frightened by the monstrous, fantastic extravagance of the scene. Silas must have decoyed her to the heart of some distorted maze, where death was not solemn, nor grief venerable; and therein she was lost. Crying, her arm crooked across her eyes, she made her way over to Linnet, who had risen to his feet. "It's soap,— *soap*," she stammered, taking refuge against him.

He held her, since no words could help, and she made herself as small as possible within his arm. Silas called out to him across the gallery, "I have thrown Gregory into the vat," pointing to the wrong vat, and forcing himself to laugh very loudly.

"But what is to become of *you*? madman!" Linnet exclaimed.

This was a new idea to Silas.

"Yes, I must think of getting away, it's true," he replied, suddenly busy; and he moved excitably in what he thought to be the direction of the door. But he had lost his bearings, and struck himself against the corner of a vat. "What's that?" he called out. "I'll have no nonsense," he added, speaking in a tone of incipient panic which he tried to cover up by menace. "There is no time to be lost; I can't be kept hanging about here, or I shall be taken. I must get away, and hide somewhere. I must hide in a barn. You will have to bring me food. The first thing to be done is to get away." All the while he was speaking he moved about, groping amongst the vats, trying to find his way out, but amongst that number, where nothing helped him to distinguish one from the other, with each step he became more confusedly lost. "I'm blind!" he cried, at last standing stock-still, and from the anguish in his voice it might have been believed that he had never made the discovery before.

Then he started to stride about, up and down, in and out of the gangways left between the vats, taking any opening that offered itself. Linnet tried to speak to him; he was interrupted, reasonable words fluttered vainly amongst the vibrant emotions with which Silas's soul was strung. Neither Linnet nor Nan could have any cognisance of such a diapason. "You shall not come near me," Silas shouted; "how am I to know you wouldn't give me up? although I killed Gregory for you; and I loved Gregory.—We've destroyed one another. It's right,—people like us ought to go. There's no place for us. I can't save myself," he said, "I'm blind; everyone can take advantage of me. How could I live hidden for weeks in the country? But I'll give them trouble first. . ."

He was full of a crazy, hopeless defiance; he turned upon them the wild flash of his sightless eyes. "It *must* end in defeat," he said, "what match is a blind man for clear-seeing men? You had me at a disadvantage, all my life,—all of you! You were orderly, while I struggled. Gone under! but not as tamely as you think." As he spoke he found the door that gave access to the outside stairs, and dragged it open, blundering out into the air on the iron landing. They saw him there, against the sky, silhouetted for a moment, before he disappeared on his reckless descent of the hazardous stair.

III

EVENING WAS RAPIDLY FALLING, BUT the coming of night would befriend him, since it could not hinder. As he reached the foot of the stair he stood for a moment in hesitation. He listened. The tessellated square was silent, but for a drip of water off a gutter into one of the great butts; no footsteps rang across the cobbles; no voice exclaimed "Why, Dene!"; no call from Nan or Linnet echoed down to him from above. He felt himself more utterly alone than ever in his life before, more finally at bay. Never for an instant did the idea of giving himself up cross his mind. He was calmer now than he had been up in the gallery, where he had bruised himself so cruelly against these serried vats. Here, at least, he had space around him; and out there, where he meant to go, would be still wider space, the flat freedom of the Fens, the sky above his head, and night, the only ally that could begin to equalise his chances with other men.

But there would be uncertainty. Always the uncertainty whether he had or had not been seen. He might be ringed about by pursuers closing in upon him, and not know it. He must make up his mind to that; he must make up his mind to the knowledge that defeat would overtake him in the end. This knowledge came to him with a strangely familiar quietness; it was as though it had been with him all his life, although he might not have given it a name.

In the silence of the evening he passed beyond the factory and gained the road on the top of the great dyke stretching across the Fens. Upon its eminence he paused, forlorn, uncertain, and derelict. That illumination which had sustained him before, seemed now to have deserted him; he no longer trod with the same assurance, but cautiously, afraid of making a false step and of slipping down the sides of the dyke, afraid of being seen, upright upon the skyline, yet not venturing to leave the road and to make his way across the flooded country. Yet as he stumbled on, he realised that therein lay his wisest course: the floods would reveal no footmarks, and he would be less conspicuous than erect on the height of the dyke. In so far as his hopelessness could devise a plan, that was the plan to follow. He struck across the road, and, crouching on his heels, allowed himself to slither down the escarpment. At the bottom he found the water, icy about his ankles, and shivered at its sinister touch. Nevertheless, he plunged forward into it, his hands outstretched before him, determined to put all possible distance between himself and Abbot's Etchery. Behind him the three chimneys of the factory vomited their black plumes of noiseless smoke that trailed across the sky, but of this he did not reckon; he was aware only of the cry of the curlew circling above him, and of the marshy ground that sucked back his steps beneath the water. He fought his way, each foot held down and his progress hampered as in a nightmare, and with an effort he dragged one foot after the other stickily out, ploughing onwards into the unknown breadth of the marshes, ignorant of his surroundings, of whether night had fallen, concealing him, or whether the last bars of day still made of him a distinguishable mark. And, for his greater misery and discomfort, as he advanced across the submerged fields, he came periodically to the ditches that were their boundaries, and knew them because his footing suddenly failed him and threw him forward into the water, pitching down upon hands and knees, so that presently he was drenched, and the touch of the water which at first had been only about his ankles now conquered his body also, little by little, penetrating to his skin, glacial as the presaged touch of death. Still he advanced, striving towards no known prospective refuge, but merely, irrationally, to increase the distance, without considering the paltriness of the help those few poor miles could afford him.

By now, although he could not be certain of it, night had fully come. A huge, low moon stole up above the horizon, and sailed slowly higher into the heavens over the flooded country. In its light the few bare trees stood up like twigs, black and stark; and still across the now shining expanse of water the blind man held on his laborious, hindered way the splash of his steps breaking the placid surface into a ripple of jet and silver. He had no notion how far he might have gone; he was uncertain even whether he had succeeded in keeping straight in the same direction. Every now and then he came to a hillock of higher ground, which lifted him for the moment out of the floods, and every now and then he stumbled into a ditch, from which he extricated himself, his teeth chattering; and all the time he walked with his hands groping before him, but they could not save him from the ditches that seemed to lie in wait for him and to take pleasure in trapping him unawares. He thought that he must have been walking half the night. Even the curlews had ceased to cry long since, and no owl hooted across the waste of waters. His extreme weariness deadened him; but fever reanimated him; and it was a conflict as to which would gain the advantage. At one moment he thought that he must sink down from exhaustion, even into the floods; the next moment, a bout of fear and determination spurred him on, and he splashed forward, behind his groping hands, while obscure mutterings came in the immense silence of the night from his moving lips.

Morning found him crouching beside some meagre trees upon one of the hillocks out of reach of the water. His hair was matted, his eyes bloodshot, his clothes wet and dankly clinging to his limbs. He crouched as closely as possible to the ground, feeling about for the shelter of the trees, which, leafless as they were, offered no shelter at all. He crept about amongst them,—they might be half a dozen in number, a small clump;—he crept over the twenty square feet or so of the little island on which he was marooned, and once or twice he seemed tempted to renew his passage through the water, for he cautiously adventured down to its edge, and stretched out his foot towards it, but, although he essayed this on different sides of the mound, he always took his foot back shuddering as soon as he encountered the water, and withdrew himself in the same shambling, furtive fashion to the shelter of the trees.

It was here that in the afternoon he was found by the men who were out for his capture. They came beating across the flooded fields in extended order, as men beating for game. When they first descried him from a little way off, he still was stealing about his patch of refuge, rambling uneasily and without purpose, now coming down to the water's edge, now out of sight over the curve of the hillock, now reappearing to slink between the trees. Uncouth, haggard, his clothes torn and soiled, his hands always at their unhappy groping, his useless eyes turning hither and thither, he resembled some half-crazy castaway that might have subsisted there for days on berries and foul water, too bemused now for further endeavour; too broken in spirit for any frenzy of despair; merely acquiescent in his climax of the long premonitory years; waiting for the end which, after all the riot and the burden, could not be otherwise than welcome.

IV

AFTER THAT DAY CLEAN APRIL poured sunlight over the marshes. Flocks of plover settled on the emerging pasture; and the sea, whose presence was divined rather than seen over the edge of the fens, ceased to be a threat, and became a promise, for the peculiar void of the sky above it, where land stopped short, grew luminous with the transparency of shower-washed spaces. The very roads, the very railway line with its straight, shining metals, streamed away, avenues of promise and escape.

Like a great bowl opened to the gold-moted emptiness of heaven the country lay, recipient of the benediction.

January–September, 1920

A Note About the Author

V. Sackville-West (1892–1952) was an English novelist, poet, journalist, and gardener. Born at Knole, the Sackville's hereditary home in west Kent, Vita was the daughter of English peer Lionel Sackville-West and his cousin Victoria, herself the illegitimate daughter of the 2nd Baron Sackville and a Spanish dancer named Pepita. Educated by governesses as a young girl, Vita later attended school in Mayfair, where she met her future lover Violet Keppel. An only child, she entertained herself by writing novels, plays, and poems in her youth, both in English and French. At the age of eighteen, she made her debut in English society and was courted by powerful and well-connected men. She had affairs with men and women throughout her life, leading an open marriage with diplomat Harold Nicholson. Following their wedding in 1913, the couple moved to Constantinople for one year before returning to settle in England, where they raised two sons. Vita's most productive period of literary output, in which she published such works as *The Land* (1926) and *All Passion Spent* (1931), coincided with her affair with English novelist Virginia Woolf, which lasted from 1925 to 1935. The success of Vita's writing—published through Woolf's Hogarth Press—allowed her lover to publish some of her masterpieces, including *The Waves* (1931) and *Orlando* (1928), the latter being inspired by Sackville-West's family history, androgynous features, and unique personality. Vita died at the age of seventy at Sissinghurst Castle, where she worked with her husband to design one of England's most famous gardens.

A Note from the Publisher

Spanning many genres, from non-fiction essays to literature classics to children's books and lyric poetry, Mint Edition books showcase the master works of our time in a modern new package. The text is freshly typeset, is clean and easy to read, and features a new note about the author in each volume. Many books also include exclusive new introductory material. Every book boasts a striking new cover, which makes it as appropriate for collecting as it is for gift giving. Mint Edition books are only printed when a reader orders them, so natural resources are not wasted. We're proud that our books are never manufactured in excess and exist only in the exact quantity they need to be read and enjoyed.

bookfinity™

Discover more of your favorite classics with Bookfinity™.

- Track your reading with custom book lists.
- Get great book recommendations for your personalized Reader Type.
- Add reviews for your favorite books.
- AND MUCH MORE!

Visit **bookfinity.com** and take the fun Reader Type quiz to get started.

Enjoy our classic and modern companion pairings!

Classic & Modern